MUTTS & MAGNOLIAS

RACHEL HANNA

CHAPTER 1

DAWSON STOOD ON THE EDGE OF THE DOCK AND flung his fishing line out into the water. One of his favorite ways to spend the day was fishing in a small local lake on the property of one of his friends.

"I keep getting it caught in the tree," Dylan lamented. Dawson swore his hook had been in more trees today than in the water.

"Let me see it... again," he said with a sigh. As calm as he normally was, he was getting frustrated. Dylan's brain didn't seem to be switched on today. He wasn't himself at all, and he hadn't been in a couple of weeks. Julie had written it off to the holiday rush that had just finished. Kids were always distracted when they had to go back to school after

Christmas. But Dawson thought there was more to it, which was why he'd taken his son fishing today.

"Thanks," Dylan said, as Dawson handed him back his pole for the umpteenth time. "What's going on, buddy?"

"What do you mean?" he asked, staring out at the water.

"You seem a little different lately."

"Maybe it's that puberty thing they've been talking to us about in health class."

Dawson chuckled. "Maybe, but it usually doesn't make you change this fast. Is something going on?"

"Nope."

Dylan was an emotional kid, but this was more than that. It was like he was keeping a secret, and Dawson didn't like it at all. With his history of being in foster care and having such a tumultuous time with his birth parents, Dawson knew there was a lot going on in his growing brain. When he didn't want to talk about it, Dawson got worried.

Of course, it wasn't like most boys were very communicative, especially at this age. He remembered how he was, and talking about his emotions wasn't exactly on the top of his list of things to do. He tried to walk that fine line with his own son, where he was available to talk but not pushy about it. Right now, he was teetering on the line of becoming pushy, so he pulled back.

"Are you enjoying school?"

Dylan tensed up a bit and tossed his rod on the ground beside him. "I'm sick of fishing. Can I go back home?"

"Son, it's miles to get home. You're going to walk?"

Dylan shrugged his shoulders. "It's hot out here."

"It's January, dude. It's not hot."

"Can I sit in the truck, then?"

Dawson wanted to ask more questions, but that seemed to be the wrong thing to do at the moment. "Sure." He tossed him the keys. "I'll get all the stuff together and come over there in a minute, okay?"

"Okay." Without another word, Dylan slowly walked toward the truck. As Dawson started gathering up the poles and tackle box, his phone buzzed in his pocket.

"Hello?"

"Hey, honey," Julie said from the other end of the line. "How's fishing?"

He laughed. "Fishing is fine, but our son is another story."

"He's still acting weird?"

"Yep. In fact, he asked to go sit in the truck. I'm getting our stuff together now."

"Did you try to talk to him?"

"I did. He definitely doesn't want to talk about whatever it is."

"Well, we can't just let it go, right? I mean, we have to find out what's going on."

Dawson sat on the tackle box. "We have to be careful here, Julie. Boys don't love talking all that much anyway, and we don't want to make him close off even further."

"What about counseling?"

He laughed. "And what would we tell the counselor? That he's being quiet and acting funny? I think they'd need more to go on than that. Plus, Dylan would shut down if we asked him to go talk to some stranger. Let's give it a little time and see if he's just having a bad couple of weeks, okay?"

"Okay. I guess," she said, begrudgingly. He knew his wife wanted to fix the situation because that's who she was. A fixer. She didn't like it when something was wrong with someone she loved and she couldn't fix it.

"Don't worry, babe. I'm on top of it. We'll figure it out."

"I trust you," she said. "Oh, a customer just came in. Let me go help them. See you at home. Love you!"

Before he could respond, the line disconnected. He looked up at the truck and could only see Dylan's silhouette. Something was definitely wrong with his boy, and he was going to make it his mission to find out what it was.

Griffin Connor stood on the front porch of his property and took in a deep breath. It'd been many years since he'd stood in this spot and stared out over the acreage his grandfather had owned for decades. The family property had been passed down several generations, and now it was his turn. He didn't want to screw it up. It was an honor. It was a responsibility. It was a huge life change.

A veterinarian, he'd left his flourishing practice behind in Nashville and come home to Seagrove, South Carolina, to take over where his late grandfather left off. The vet practice that his grandfather had built from the ground up forty years ago was now his, along with four acres, an office building and a house. This place that he'd loved all his life was now his, and he was terrified.

Griffin hadn't grown up in Seagrove, although he'd visited it a million times as a little kid. He had vivid memories of floating through the marshes on his grandfather's rickety little boat and eating shrimp and grits at the local waterfront cafe.

He'd lived in nearby Charleston as a kid, but when his parents divorced, his mother had taken him to Tennessee to be closer to her family. His father eventually remarried and moved to Oklahoma to be near his new wife's family, leaving Griffin to feel abandoned.

The one constant in his life, besides his mother, was his grandfather. Everybody called him Doc, although Griffin had called him Papa Doc. He was a tall, lanky man with white hair and the biggest smile Griffin had ever seen. Papa Doc had been his light in every stormy time of his life, and he missed him more than he could express now.

After a quick battle with cancer, he was gone, leaving everything he had to Griffin. Of course, he was his closest living relative, with Griffin's mom having passed away years ago. Doc had always been so proud that Griffin followed in his footsteps and graduated from The University of Georgia's revered veterinary school. Even back then, he'd wanted Griffin to come work with him in Seagrove, but

Griffin had been young and idealistic, and he wanted to start his own practice in Nashville.

Although he loved his old practice, there was a part of him that wished he had come to Seagrove all those years ago just so he could've soaked up as much of his grandfather's wisdom as he could.

"Dr. Connor, is there anything else I can do for you?"

He turned to Sam, the young man he'd hired to help him unload his truck full of furniture, and smiled. "No, you've helped me a lot today. Here you go." He pulled a wad of cash out of his pocket and gave it to the teenager.

Sam stared down at the money. "No, sir, I couldn't take this much money from you. My momma would kill me."

Griffin laughed. "A man needs money in his pocket. And you deserve it. You've worked hard today."

"Thank you, sir."

As he watched Sam get into his little pickup truck, complete with rust on the sides, he remembered those early years of struggling through college. Back then, he wished he'd had a truck at all. His mother worked hard as a teacher, and Papa Doc had helped as much as his mother would allow. In the end, Griffin knew he had to earn his way in the world and pay his dues.

He walked down into the yard and over to the office. This was where Papa Doc saw his patients every day. He treated dogs, cats, pet rabbits and just about anything else that came through the door. He was also trained in treating larger animals and often made house calls to treat horses. Griffin wasn't trained in that, so he'd just be handling mostly dogs and cats.

Ironically, he didn't have a dog of his own. That was the first order of business now that his things were moved. He'd be heading to the local shelter to find a new best friend. Being in a town where he knew no one would not be easy. He had no idea whether his grandfather's patients would stay with him or go to the other vet in town.

There was a certain amount of stress that came along with leaving his whole life behind in Nashville and coming to take over Papa Doc's business. What if he'd let his old life go for nothing? What if he ruined his grandfather's business and ended up having to sell everything? Okay, maybe he was being a bit dramatic.

Still, leaving Nashville had been hard. There were a lot of memories there, both good and bad. Every corner seemed to hold memories of some kind, but it was familiar, and right now nothing looked or felt familiar.

He stepped into the office and sat down behind the desk Papa Doc had used since Griffin was a little boy. All worn and wooden, he could see gouges where little dog and cat nails had probably clawed it up. Nothing stayed pristine in a veterinarian's office.

He opened each drawer, pulling out various items his grandfather had kept. Many were antiquated and wouldn't be used today, but he did things the old-fashioned way. *"Griff, sometimes the old ways are the best ways. You don't always need to reinvent the wheel. The old one works just fine!"*

Griffin smiled as he closed all but one drawer. He looked down and saw a blue envelope with his name on it. He retrieved a silver letter opener from the desktop and slid it under the flap of the envelope.

As soon as he opened it and pulled out the yellowed piece of paper, he could smell Papa Doc's cologne. It was like he'd just appeared in the room, with his requisite pipe and plaid shirt.

Dear Griff,

Well, I suppose if you're reading this, I'm living it up in heaven. I can't wait to see your grandma, your momma and everybody who went before me.

But that also means my beloved patients will be left without a doctor, and I just can't have that. I hope you'll take over my practice and my property, Griff. You're a talented vet, and you know I've always wanted you to come to Seagrove. I think this place is your real home, and I believe you'll see that in time.

I love you, buddy. The best parts of my life included you, and I will always watch over you. Do good things. Find someone who truly loves you like I did, and your life will be so much fuller.

I'm rooting for you, always.

Love,

Papa Doc

Griffin wiped the tears from his eyes. Papa Doc had always been more on the gruff side, so this wasn't a letter he ever expected to read from him. He was a tough old Marine, so showing a lot of emotion hadn't been his "thing".

He folded the paper, put it back in the envelope, and placed it into the drawer. He decided he would keep it there to read on those days when he didn't believe in himself or just needed a little encouragement.

Griffin had to smile when he read the part about finding love. Papa Doc had been on him for years about finding a wife. He'd come close once, almost getting engaged to Paulina. But when she'd cheated on him with her co-worker, that relationship ended and Griffin opted to only love his patients from now on. Dogs never let you down. They always loved you, no matter what. Cats? Well, it really depended on the cat in question he'd found.

"Great class, everybody!" Janine said, waving as her students filed out of the building. If she was being honest with herself, she was exhausted. After getting married, she and William bought their first place together, a beautiful condo overlooking the marsh, right near the yoga studio. She'd moved out of Julie's old cottage. While Colleen still lived there, she and Tucker were on an extended work trip out west, which meant that Julie had to rent out the place on a short-term lease. The couple that lived there seemed nice enough, from what Janine could tell.

Blending their lives was more challenging than Janine had imagined. Of course, she and William had known each other for a good while, so nothing about his habits had surprised her much. Still, each of them had their own stuff, and she'd found they each did things very differently. For instance, she liked to wash all the dishes right after eating dinner, while William preferred to "let them soak" and get to them in the morning.

Then there was the toilet paper issue. How had she never noticed he put the toilet paper roll on backwards? Everybody knew you pulled it down from the front.

Of course, these were minor issues, and she was thrilled to finally be married to the man of her dreams. Waking up next to him, snuggling with him on a rainy afternoon, watching movies… they were all things she'd dreamed of her whole life. God had blessed her with a man who loved her, and she would never take that for granted.

"Are you still open?"

Janine turned around and saw a young, very pregnant girl standing in the doorway of her studio. "Yes, of course! Come on in. I'm Janine, the owner."

She smiled slightly. "I'm Tabatha."

It took Janine a moment before her name registered. "Oh, from Abigail and Celeste's house?"

"Yeah."

"It's nice to finally meet you. How can I help you?"

"Do you work with pregnant women?"

Janine nodded. "All the time. Yoga is very helpful for pregnant women. What issues are you having?"

She reached around to her lower back. "It hurts here all the time. And my right hip hurts when I sit or when I sleep. Basically, everything hurts." Her face fell, and she sighed. Janine seemed to remember Tabatha was sixteen years old, from what Julie had said.

"I can imagine this is a hard time for you. I'd be glad to help you however I can. I have a class for pregnant women…"

"No."

"No?"

"I don't want to be in a class with other women." She looked down at her feet.

"Oh. Can I ask why? I mean, they're all going through the same thing…"

"No, they're not. They probably wanted their babies. And I bet most of them are married. I'm sixteen years old, and this is embarrassing. I didn't ask for this." Her face was turning redder and redder, and a stray tear escaped from her eye.

Janine walked closer and put her hand on Tabatha's shoulder. "You're right. If you don't feel comfortable being in a class, how about I give you some private sessions? I can teach you the moves to do to help relieve your pain. Does that work?"

She looked up at Janine. "Really? You'd do that for me? Why?"

"Because in Seagrove, we help each other."

"But I don't have enough money to pay for private lessons."

Janine smiled. "It's fine. I can work with you in between my other classes. I'm here anyway."

"Thank you!" Tabatha said, tears still in her eyes. "This has just been so hard."

"Consider it my gift to you. Now, why don't we take a look at my calendar and see when we can get started? Sound good?"

"A dog? What are we going to do with a dog?" Celeste asked, her arms crossed.

Abigail stared at her. "Why do we need to *do* something with a dog? Can't we just have a dog?"

"I mean, I have nothing against dogs, but we have a lot going on here between hosting the foster camps and..."

"And what? We don't do anything else," Abigail said, laughing.

Thanks to the generosity of Elaine Benson, they were both able to get acclimated to Seagrove for a few months before figuring out what they wanted to do for work.

"Besides, I'm sure Ben wouldn't be too happy having a dog running around this place. He's running his practice here, and it wouldn't be very professional."

"Oh, I don't know about that. I think a dog might class up the joint," Ben said, walking up behind her.

She squinted her eyes at him. "I thought you were in with a patient?"

He smiled and kissed her cheek. "I was. She just left, lollipop in hand and grin on her face. Now, what's this about a dog?"

"I was telling Celeste that the local shelter is bursting at the seams. They had an article about it in the newspaper. I'd like to go take a look and maybe get a dog that needs a home. Celeste is being a grinch about it, as per usual."

Celeste rolled her eyes. "I'm being realistic. Who's going to take care of this dog?"

"Me," Abigail said.

"And I'll help when I'm here," Ben interjected.

"I'm sure Tabatha will help, too. She loves dogs."

"I like dogs too, but it's going to be a lot of

responsibility with a pregnant teenager, a doctor's office and a bunch of teenage foster kids."

Ben chuckled. "Celeste, stop thinking of reasons it won't work, and think about some adorable pooch over there in a kennel, waiting for a new home. *This* home."

"Don't you try to guilt me, Ben Callaway!" she said, poking him in the side. "Okay, fine. But no big dogs that drool and shed everywhere. Get something reasonable."

"I'll keep those parameters in mind," Abigail said, rushing out of the house before Celeste would change her mind.

CHAPTER 2

JANINE SAT ON THE EDGE OF THE DOCK, WAITING FOR William to get back from his last tour of the day. This one was a group of tourists who were very excited to see the marshes and learn more about local wildlife. It made Janine smile every time she thought about how excited William was about his job. He had really come a long way from when they'd first met, and he'd been so unhappy with his life.

"Hey, gorgeous. Do you have a boyfriend?" he said, as he slowly steered the boat toward the dock. She assumed he'd dropped his group off at the other dock since he was alone.

"Nope. I'm free as a bird," she said, leaning back and laughing, her toes dangling precariously over the water. She tried not to think about the creepy crawlies and alligators that could be lurking below.

"To what do I owe this pleasure? I thought we were meeting for an early dinner?" He tied off the boat and stepped out, sitting down beside her.

She kissed him on the cheek and put her head on his shoulder. "I was just missing you."

"Why do I feel like there's something else?"

"The adoption agency called," she said with a sigh.

"I take it that's not good news?"

Janine sat up and looked at him. "We got passed over again. They said they preferred a younger couple."

It wasn't like Janine was at retirement age, but she was in her late forties. So far, every pregnant woman said she was a little too old for a baby. They wanted their kids to have younger parents. She tried not to judge the courageous birth mothers who were giving up their babies for better lives than they could give them, but sometimes she just wanted to scream.

"Honey, it'll work itself out. We just have to be patient. I mean, we've only been married for a few months."

Janine smiled. "I know. I'm just ready to finally be

a mother and build a family with you. I can't wait to see you be a dad."

"I can't wait to see you be a mom. You're going to be exceptional, Janine."

"I sure hope so."

"So, what else did you do today?"

"Taught a gazillion classes, of course. Oh, and I also met Tabatha, the girl staying with Abigail and Celeste."

"The pregnant teenager? How'd you meet her?"

"She came to the studio with some pain. I've offered to give her some private lessons for free."

"Really?"

"Yeah. I feel bad for her. Can you imagine being pregnant at her age and how scared she must be? And not only that, but she's in foster care. She must feel very alone in the world. Abigail and Celeste are helping her so much, but it's not like having parents to love and protect you."

"Very true. I think it's great that you offered her some free lessons. That's why I love you, Janine. You're good to the core." He kissed the top of her head.

"Well, I hope a birth mother thinks we're both so wonderful that she entrusts her baby to us."

He smiled. "It will happen, sweetie. I know it will."

Abigail stood in front of the row of cages and sighed. "They're all so cute!"

Sadie, the nice young woman who volunteered at the animal shelter, chuckled. "It's hard working here because I want to take them all home."

The volume in the kennel area was so loud from dogs barking that Abigail could hardly hear her. She looked up and down the row again, trying to decide. It didn't help that each dog looked at her like they were begging to be taken home, but Celeste would literally kill her while she slept if she brought home more than one.

She knew she didn't want a larger dog just because it would be harder to contain in the house. She'd already called a fencing company to come out and give them estimates on fencing in the backyard, but until then there would be lots of long dog walks in her future.

"That one is adorable," she said, pointing at a brown and white spotted dog on the end.

"That's Bingo. He came in as a stray a couple of weeks ago."

"Aren't you just adorable?" Abigail said, rubbing the top of his head through the chain link. "He's just a little big, I think. My roommate would have a fit."

"We do have some puppies that just came in. They appear to be full-blooded Beagles."

"Really?"

"They're just over in our puppy room down the hall."

"Sadie, we need you out back for a meet and greet," a man said, poking his head through the doorway.

"Be right there."

"Meet and greet?"

"It's when someone brings their dog from home to meet a dog they're thinking of adopting here. Do you mind checking out the puppies on your own?"

Abigail smiled. "A room full of puppies? Sign me up! You might have to kick me out when you close later."

Sadie laughed before disappearing out the back door. Abigail scratched Bingo's head one more time before walking toward the puppy room. She felt bad not adopting him, but she felt good that the shelter was no-kill, which meant he'd find a home no matter what.

She walked down the hall and into the puppy room, but there was only one Beagle left in the kennel. She hurried over and opened it, putting the puppy straight up to her face and kissing its cheek.

"Oh my gosh, you're just the cutest thing I've ever seen!" She looked at the collar and saw the puppy's name - Petunia. How perfect! "You're coming home with me."

"Excuse me, but you're holding my puppy." Abigail turned to see a man standing there, staring at her. He was holding his wallet in his hand and looking at her like she'd just tried to mug him.

"What?"

"I was planning to get that puppy, but then I realized I left my wallet in my car."

"Did you tell the staff you wanted this puppy?"

"Well, no. Not yet."

"Did you fill out paperwork?"

"Again, not yet." She could tell he was getting frustrated with her.

She pulled the puppy closer like she was holding onto the most expensive thing in the world. "Then it seems to me you just visited a puppy and claimed it as your own… *in your mind*."

"Look, I'm tired, and I just want to get my puppy and go home. Now, please, hand her to me."

"No."

"Listen, I have a nice big property, and I'm even a…"

"And I have a nice big house on the beach, so we're even." Abigail brushed past him and walked toward the door.

"You're not being very nice."

"As I see it, you simply decided in your brain that you wanted this particular puppy, but you didn't tell the staff, and you didn't fill out papers. How do I know you were even in here before me? You could've lied about that."

"What? Why would I lie about that?"

"I don't know you from Adam's housecat, sir. But what I do know is this puppy is coming home with me today. I love her already."

"So, what am I supposed to do?"

She shrugged her shoulders. "Take Bingo home. He's next door, and he's adorable. I think you'll make a great couple."

"How are you feeling today?" Celeste asked Tabatha as she finished making a sandwich for each of them. Dinner tonight was basic, at best. Abigail had gone off to the animal shelter and would probably return with five dogs and an orphaned goat.

"Fat and gassy."

She set the sandwich in front of Tabatha. "Sorry I asked."

"I never want to be pregnant again," she groaned.

"I'm sure one day you'll change your mind when you're older and more settled. This wasn't exactly what you had planned. Speaking of that, have you made any decisions..."

"No, and I wish everybody would stop asking me."

Celeste paused for a moment, taking a bite of her sandwich. "Tabatha, you're running out of time. If you plan on raising this baby, we need to decorate a nursery, get you some help with financial support, make plans about daycare..."

"I know," she groaned, picking at her sandwich.

"And if you opt for adoption, we need to meet with the agency so you can start looking at families."

"I know, Celeste!" She pounded her fist on the table and then descended into tears. "Don't you know how hard this is for me?"

Celeste sighed and put her sandwich on her plate. "No, I don't know. And I'm sorry if it seems like I'm pressuring you because that's not what I'm trying to do. I just know that you could have this baby in another few weeks, and I don't want you to feel the pressure then. You'd have to make a hasty decision that you might regret, and this is hard enough without the added pressure once a baby is here."

She wiped her eyes with a paper towel and nodded. "I know you're right. I just don't know what to do."

"Do you think it might help to talk to someone?"

"Like a therapist?"

"Yes. Maybe somebody with no connection to you could help you look at the pros and cons, and make the right decision for you and the baby."

"I think that sounds like a good idea, but I don't know anybody."

"I'll ask around, okay?"

Tabatha looked at her, tears welling in her eyes. "I don't know what I'd do without you and Abigail. At least I feel like I have family."

Celeste reached over and squeezed her hand. "You do have family, and we'll be here for you no matter what, okay?"

"Okay."

Abigail pulled into the driveway as Petunia scurried around the front seat, looking for anything to get into. She'd forgotten how energetic puppies tend to be, and now she was wondering if she'd gotten in over her head. This was going to be like having an infant, and she was pretty sure she was going to be cleaning up a lot of accidents in the near future.

Even though she wanted a dog, she had still been in decision mode when "that man" came into the kennel and irritated her. The nerve of him thinking he could stake a claim on a puppy just because he thought about adopting it. Her stubborn nature - a side of her she rarely let slip out - had come out full force, and now she felt a little silly for how she'd reacted.

Petunia was adorable, though. She was playful, rambunctious and the cuddliest thing Abigail had ever seen. Hopefully, Celeste felt the same way.

"We're home, little girl! Let's go meet the family," she said, picking her up. She needed to go buy a kennel and bedding before the stores closed, or Petunia might be sleeping in her bed.

As she walked up to the front door, she wondered what Celeste was going to say. Ben had softened her a bit, but Celeste was still Celeste, through and through. She would definitely say whatever was on her mind.

Abigail opened the door and found Ben standing next to his office door, locking up. "Oh, my goodness! Look at this little one!" He reached out for the puppy and took her, giving her a kiss on top of her head. Petunia wiggled in his arms.

"Isn't she adorable? Her name is Petunia."

He held her up and looked at her. "I'm not sure how, but she looks like a Petunia."

"Right? Where's Celeste?"

"In the kitchen with Tabatha. I think they've been having an emotional conversation, so I didn't want to interrupt."

"Maybe not the best time to introduce them to Petunia?"

He shrugged his shoulders. "Maybe meeting her will take the edge off." Ben handed the puppy back to Abigail.

Before she could head toward the kitchen, Celeste appeared in the doorway with Tabatha right behind her. "I knew you couldn't come back without a dog."

"I told you I was going to adopt one."

She laughed. "I know, but I thought it would take you longer than half an hour to choose our new family member."

It felt funny to hear Celeste refer to them as family, given the tumultuous relationship they'd had since childhood. She opted not to make a joke. Sometimes it was better not to poke at Celeste.

"This is Petunia."

Tabatha's eyes lit up. "She is adorable!" She walked over and picked up the puppy, kissing her on the nose. "She can sleep with me."

Abigail shook her head. "No way. We're training this little girl from the beginning. I do need to run to the store and get her a kennel, some bedding, food…"

"Well, then, she can stay with me until you get back. I need some practice taking care of another living creature, anyway."

Tabatha hadn't told them much about her plans for the baby, and they had decided not to push too much. But the time was getting closer, and they still didn't know whether she was going to keep the baby and try to raise him or her, or if she was going to pursue adoption.

She was a sixteen-year-old girl, of course, and

that meant her emotions were already all over the place. Add in the hormonal fluctuations of pregnancy, and she was often an emotional mess. Abigail wasn't sure how she would ever be able to raise a baby on her own without an education or a job, but she also knew that she and Celeste would be there no matter what.

"Okay, you keep her with you until I get back," Abigail said, starting to turn toward the door. She looked back at Petunia and saw Celeste rubbing the top of her head. "Looks like somebody likes Petunia," she said, grinning.

"I have to be present in her life or else she might end up acting like you," Celeste shot back, stifling a smile.

Griffin stood in front of the wall of dog food bags and felt like his veterinary education was lacking. Surely he should be able to choose the right one for his new dog, but they all looked alike, and they all had so many ingredients. For a moment, he thought about looking up one of those natural dog food recipes, but he also knew he wouldn't have time to do that.

After finally choosing a bag of food, he walked over to the section with kennels and bedding. Bingo was a larger dog than he was planning to get, so he would need a kennel for him to stay in when Griffin wasn't home. He reached up and took the last large kennel and a matching pillow bed. As he placed them into his cart, he turned to see the same woman he saw at the animal shelter.

"Well, if it isn't the puppy snatcher herself," he said dryly, before turning back to his cart.

"Puppy snatcher? Petunia wasn't yours."

"I told you I was just going to get my wallet." This woman was infuriating, partly because of what she'd done and partly because he found her to be very attractive.

"You can't call dibs on a puppy and then walk outside." She reached up and pulled on a smaller kennel, obviously struggling to get it down. Griffin wanted to offer to help, but he was still aggravated at this woman and wanted to see her struggle for just a second. Unfortunately, she yanked on it one good time, and down it came. Griffin closed the gap between them and caught the heavy box when it was within a couple of inches of knocking her right in the head.

He held the box up as she jumped out of the way

and then placed it into her cart. "I assume you want this one?"

She cleared her throat. "Yes. Thank you. I appreciate you catching that before it, you know, killed me."

Griffin laughed. "Well, even if you did steal my puppy, I didn't want you to die over it."

"I didn't steal your… You know what, never mind. I said thank you, and I meant it. And, from your own cart, I see that it all worked out. You found another dog?"

"I did. Bingo."

She smiled broadly, and she had a nice smile. Too nice. "You adopted Bingo?"

"I did. You were right that he's a cool dog, so I took him home."

"Well, I'm glad to hear that. See? It was meant to be."

Griffin rolled his eyes. "Enjoy your puppy," he said, as he started wheeling his cart in another direction.

"You too!"

CHAPTER 3

"WHEN WILL COLLEEN BE BACK?" DIXIE ASKED AS SHE helped Julie stock the shelves in the self-help section of the bookstore.

"She and Tucker are at a toy convention in Pittsburgh right now, and I think they have another one in Sacramento after that."

"Wow, that's a lot of traveling!"

"Not for younger folks. They seem to love this new life on the road, although I miss them something fierce."

"I know you do. All those years I didn't see my William were awful, but at least you have a strong relationship with your girls."

"I am blessed to have two beautiful daughters and an adorable granddaughter."

"How are Meg and Christian?"

"Busy young, working parents. You know how it goes."

Dixie took the last book from the box and placed it on the shelf. "Time sure does pass quickly. It doesn't seem like that many years ago that Johnny and I were those same young parents. You don't realize it until you get older how precious those moments are." Her eyes welled with tears. Something about getting older made her more emotional.

"How's Harry doing?"

"Great. He's working on the raised flower beds in the backyard. Gives him something to do."

"Sometimes we need to give our husbands something to do, right?" Julie said, laughing.

"So, Dawson told me y'all have been having some trouble with Dylan lately?"

"He's acting strange. He wants to be alone a lot, and his personality has changed."

"Do you think maybe he's thinking about his birth mom?"

Julie broke down the empty box and tossed it into the back room for recycling. "Maybe. I guess it's possible, although we have an open dialogue about her. He was fine during the holidays, but as soon as he went back to school, things changed."

"Well, then, maybe something is going on at school?"

Julie looked at her for a long moment. "You know what? You're probably right. I think I'll make an appointment with his teacher and see if she knows of anything that might be going on."

"Good idea."

"Do you mind if I go make that call now? I'll just step outside."

Dixie waved her hand. "Of course. Go right ahead. I'll finish up here."

She watched Julie go outside and smiled to herself. She'd never had a daughter of her own, but having Julie around - and now Janine as her daughter-in-law - had blessed her in ways she couldn't express.

Her cup truly overflowed with blessings, and she would always be grateful for the people in her life and the town of Seagrove.

"Okay, stretch your arms high above your head... Really reach up.... Now, slightly bend to your right..." Janine had been coaching Tabatha all morning between her other classes. During the downtime, Tabatha would study for her GED in the break room. She had to give it to the kid - she was focused on her future and determined to make something of her life.

"Wow. I really feel that on my side."

"Good. That will help you. Why don't you try the cat-cow pose again?"

"The one where I get on all fours and arch my back?"

"That's the one."

Tabatha moaned. "That one is hard with this giant belly of mine." She sat down on the floor and sighed. "I have about six weeks left, but I don't know how this can grow any more." She looked down and rubbed her hand across her stomach.

Janine sat down on the floor next to her. "Do you know the sex?"

"No. I didn't want to find out."

"Really? I think that would drive me crazy! I would buy all sorts of stuff..." Janine could literally feel her foot wedged in her mouth. "I'm sorry."

"Sorry for what?"

"I mean, I don't know your situation. I'm sure buying a bunch of stuff isn't easy right now."

Tabatha smiled. "It's okay. I know it's weird to be

my age and hugely pregnant. I didn't ask for this either."

"I know."

"Do you have any kids?"

Janine shook her head. "No, but we're trying to adopt. It's not working out well so far, but we're not giving up. I didn't meet the right guy until it was too late for me to have children biologically."

"Do you think you'll love a kid that's not your own?"

"Absolutely! My sister and her husband adopted a young boy from foster care, and they love him fiercely. I do too. Blood doesn't mean anything."

"I guess you're right. I'm just struggling to make this decision."

"Decision?"

"I don't know if I can raise this baby. I'm just a kid myself, and I don't even have parents of my own. I'm thinking about adoption, but it seems so hard to give up my own child. Doesn't that make me a bad person?"

"I think birth mothers are some of the bravest people on Earth, actually. I don't want to tell you what to do, Tabatha, but I do believe that you're strong enough to handle whatever choice you make. If you choose to raise your baby, it's because you love him or her. If you choose to go the adoption route, it's because you love him or her. The love always stays the same."

"Thanks."

"Now, don't think I've forgotten that you need to do the cat-cow pose. Come on."

She groaned. "Fine..."

Celeste sat on the back deck overlooking the ocean and closed her eyes. She loved feeling the ocean breeze on her face on a sunny afternoon, but it was even better when Ben was sitting beside her.

"How was your day?" she asked as they sipped on glasses of wine.

"Interesting as always. I had a kid with a marble stuck in his nostril..."

"How big was that kid's nostril?" Celeste asked, laughing.

"Big enough. Then I had a mother panicking because her daughter won't eat enough vegetables. Oh, and there was a young girl who decided that climbing a tree in flip-flops was a good idea."

"Ouch."

"Yeah, it was pretty gnarly. How was your day?"

She sighed. "Uneventful, as usual. Well, except for Petunia keeping us up all night with her howling. Who knew Beagles howled?"

"Um, everyone?"

She laughed. "Apparently Abigail didn't get the memo. I finally put on my noise cancelling headphones and fell asleep to the sounds of the forest while Abigail dealt with her new daughter."

"Has she taken the dog to the vet yet?"

"No. She said she has an appointment tomorrow, though. Maybe he can give her some idea of how to get Petunia to sleep through the night and not pee on all of our rugs."

"You love her, and you know it."

"Maybe just a little. Who doesn't love a puppy, though?"

"Serial killers?"

"I think they still love puppies."

"So, I've been thinking."

"About?"

He looked over at her. "What are we doing here, Celeste?"

"Drinking wine and making jokes?"

"Look, I'm not getting any younger, so I've learned to just cut to the chase and not beat around the bush."

"Ick. That was a lot of cliches for one sentence, Ben."

"I'm being serious."

She turned her chair slightly so she could see his face. Ben wasn't often so serious, and she was a little worried about where this conversation was going. "What's going on?"

"We've been hanging out like a couple of teenagers for months now, Celeste. I guess what I want to know is whether you're interested in a real adult relationship?"

She swallowed hard, wishing she had more wine in her glass. Having grown up without parents and constantly on the defensive, she hadn't learned how to have these kinds of conversations. She hadn't learned how to lean on someone else. Easy, no frills types of relationships were her favorites.

"I'm not sure what you mean."

"Come on, Celeste. You know how this goes. Every day, we see each other in the hallway or the foyer. We wave and chat. We might even have lunch together, and sometimes dinner, usually here at the house. Weekends come, and I might come by for breakfast, or you might see me on the sidewalk. But we aren't really dating, are we?"

"Why do we have to call it something, Ben? Why does it have to be this big production?"

"Because we're adults. I'm not interested in a part-time girlfriend. I'm not interested in occasional meals and chats in the foyer. I want a girlfriend that I can take to a fancy restaurant or out dancing or to a museum."

"Gag. A museum? What kind of date is that?"

He smiled slightly. "Fine, we'll scrap the museum idea for now. I guess I wonder if you feel the same about me as I do about you?"

She paused for a moment. "I think I do."

"You think?"

"Well, I don't know how you feel about me, so how can I say it's the same?"

Now it was his turn to pause for a moment. "I really, really like you. I find myself thinking about you all day long."

"You should really focus on your patients more."

"Stop making jokes."

"Sorry."

"I want more, Celeste."

"Okay…"

"I want dates. I want to make future plans with you."

"And if I'm not ready for future plans?"

He chuckled. "Then I'll settle for real dates."

"Without museums, though."

"Noted."

Celeste smiled. It felt good to have someone really want to be with her. And it felt terrifying. Absolutely terrifying. "I'm not great at planning dates, so I'm going to leave that ball in your court."

"I'm great at it, so don't you worry about that."

She was worried about all of it. She didn't want to break Ben's heart. She didn't want to break her own heart. Long term relationships were as scary to her as a rattlesnake slithering into her path, but relationships seemed far more likely to bite her.

Abigail parked her car and walked around to retrieve Petunia from the passenger seat. She was a ball of energy, ready to bolt at any moment, so she secured a harness to her before attaching it to a leash.

Of course, as soon as she set her on the ground, Petunia pulled in every direction, trying to get detached from what she considered a medieval torture device.

"No, Petunia, come this way. This way!" she

begged as she continued to pull her toward the front door of the vet's office. Julie had kindly referred her to this place, telling her that the old doctor who used to run it had passed away, but some new doctor had taken over.

Right now, she was just glad to be somewhere that knew about dogs because she didn't. She'd never had a dog in her life, and the lack of sleep and constant "accidents" in the house were about to drive her over the edge already.

As they moved toward the door, she noticed a newly installed wooden sign that said "Dr. Griffin Connor, DVM". She opened the door and dragged Petunia inside. It was a nice enough little office, built like a log home on the outside, but much more modern in the waiting area. There was a small fish tank on one wall, and pictures of animals on another wall. There was a small front desk area, but no one was there. She rang the little silver bell and sat down to wait.

A moment later, a man walked behind the counter wearing a white doctor's jacket. He was turned the other direction at first, so she stood up to wait for him to turn around and greet her. When he did, she wanted to run in the other direction.

"Wow. Did you come here to return my beloved

puppy?" He had a quirk of a smile on his face, indicating he was making a joke.

"Never. So, let me get this straight. You're the town veterinarian?"

"One of two, actually. But I'm the better one."

"Of course you'd say that," she said, rolling her eyes.

"I graduated from the University of Georgia, one of the best vet schools in the country. The other guy graduated from clown college."

She couldn't help but laugh at how he said all of that with a straight face. "So, I take it you're Doctor Griffin Connor."

He nodded. "And I take it you're..." he looked down at his scheduling book, stared at it for a moment and turned the page. "Well, it seems I don't know who you are, actually."

"Quite a business you've made for yourself here."

"This was my grandfather's business for decades. He recently passed away, and I just took it over. Petunia is my first patient here, in fact."

"I'm sorry to hear about your grandfather."

"Thanks. Truthfully, he never had any office staff, but I desperately need a front desk person because I obviously don't know what I'm doing. So, what's your name?"

"Abigail Clayton."

He held out his hand. "Nice to meet you, Abigail."

She shook his hand and noticed how warm it was. Every doctor she'd ever known had cold hands. And he had dimples. Two of them. Deep ones that made her feel a bit swoony. She hated that she found him to be handsome because she also found him to be annoying.

"Follow me," he said, walking from behind the counter with an iPad in his hand.

"Did your grandfather use iPads here?"

He laughed. "Never in a million years. Papa Doc was not known for his technological skills. Everything was done with real pen and paper. I'm trying to digitize all of his files, but that's going to take a long time, thus the need for help around here." He flipped the light on in the exam room and pointed for her to put Petunia up on the table.

"Papa Doc?"

He smiled. "I know it sounds weird for a man my age to call him Papa Doc, but that's what I called him. Everybody in Seagrove just called him Doc."

"Ah, I see."

"So, how is my stolen daughter dog doing so far?"

She rolled her eyes. "Stop saying I stole her! You know that's not true."

"Fine," he said, laughing. "Plus, I do love Bingo. He's a crazy little fella, but he's working out just fine."

"Where is he?" she asked, looking around.

"He's in the fenced area out back. This property is several acres, so there's lots of room for him to run."

"So you live here too?"

"Yep. The house is next door. We have a pasture, a barn, and some other random buildings. Doc was thinking about opening a kennel where people could board their dogs, but..."

"You need help for that."

"Right."

"Well, I'm sure you'll figure it out soon enough," she said, wanting him to get on with the examination so she could get out of there sooner.

"I'm assuming Miss Petunia needs her next set of shots?"

"Yes. And I need to know how to get her to stop peeing on everything, and how to stop keeping me up at all hours of the night. Oh, and how to walk on a leash."

"You realize I'm not a dog trainer, right?"

She laughed. "Yes, I do. But I thought maybe you'd have some tips?"

"Fine. I'll share some of my super secret tips with you after we do the exam. Sound good?"

"Yes. Thanks."

He spent the next few minutes checking on Petunia. He looked in her ears, felt her belly, and looked at her teeth. "She appears to be about six months old."

"How can you tell?"

"Her teeth."

"Interesting. If I show you my teeth, can you tell my age?" Why did she say that? It sounded weird and creepy. She wanted to slink down to the floor.

"I don't do humans," he said, slightly smiling. He reached for the first shot he was giving Petunia and pulled up the skin on the back of her neck before injecting it. She didn't flinch.

"So, are you brand new out of college?"

"Oh no. I had my own practice in Nashville for years before Papa Doc died. He left me all of this, but I had a choice about what to do with it. I decided I couldn't let his legacy die."

"Even if it meant giving up your own legacy?" Again, she wanted to slide to the ground. Why was she getting so personal with this guy?

He shrugged his shoulders. "I guess I didn't think

of it like that, but thanks for giving me something to cause insomnia tonight."

"Sorry."

He picked up Petunia and hugged her to his chest. "I'm sorry you have to go home with this awful lady. You could've lived here in doggy heaven."

She reached over and took the puppy. "But then Bingo wouldn't have this place to call home."

"Very true."

"So, are you going to give me those super secret tips about getting her to sleep through the night?"

He leaned in close to her ear, and she could feel the warmth of his breath against her cheek. "Wear her out during the day, and she'll sleep at night," he whispered. Why did that seem so incredibly sexy?

She stepped back. "That's your ingenious plan? Run her around during the day?"

"Hey, it works. Give it a try before you knock it down."

"Fine. I will. But I'm not paying extra for that."

Julie sat nervously at the small desk. Dylan's teacher, Mrs. Hamphill, was very nice, but sitting in a classroom brought back all of her own insecurities from her youth. Something about sitting there waiting to talk to his teacher was making her unusually nervous. Maybe it was because she didn't want to hear upsetting news about her son.

"So sorry to keep you waiting!" Mrs. Hamphill breezed into the room in a frenzy, her energy far exceeding Julie's.

"No problem. I know this is a busy place. Thank you so much for seeing me so quickly."

The teacher sat down at her desk and blew out a breath. "Today has been a whirlwind. As you may know, we're preparing for the spring talent show, and I have about forty kids all trying to practice their talents in the same gymnasium. Whew! It's a chorus of just plain bad sounds in there."

Julie laughed. "I can imagine."

"So, what brings you to see me today?"

"Well, it's about my son, Dylan. He seems to be struggling with something lately, and we can't figure out what it is."

"Struggling?"

"His personality has changed completely since coming back from winter break. He's almost sullen, and he wants to spend a lot of time alone. He is more snappy toward us, and he almost seems depressed. My husband thinks suggesting therapy is going too far too fast and will probably stress Dylan out further, so I wanted to come chat with you to see if you've noticed anything."

She thought for a moment. "Well, I only see Dylan twice a day in homeroom and then history class. He moves around to other teachers in our pod all day. I haven't noticed anything particularly concerning, but I have twenty-five other kids in class most of the time. Would it help if I talk with his other teachers and see if any of them have noticed anything? I mean, if nothing else, we can keep a closer eye on him."

Julie smiled gratefully. "Yes, that would be wonderful. Thank you so much!"

"It's no problem. We want Dylan to excel. He's a great kid."

"Thank you," Julie said, standing up. "I don't want to take up any more of your time, but if there's ever anything I can do for you, please let me know."

"Do you happen to know how to make forty kids actually have talent that we can showcase?"

Julie laughed. "I'm not a magician, unfortunately."

CHAPTER 4

JANINE SAT AT HER DESK, HER PHONE IN HER HAND. She always put it on speakerphone when she was alone, just so she didn't have to hold it up to her ear.

"I'm so sorry, Janine. I really am."

"I just don't understand it. We'd offer a wonderful home for a child."

"I agree! And I know the right birthmother will come along." She was talking with their adoption agency representative, Helena, about the birthmother who hadn't chosen them.

"I just don't get it. It's not like I'm ancient."

"There are just a lot of couples waiting to adopt right now, and your age and the fact that you two just got married seems to be putting you at the bottom of the list. I know your time will come, Janine. I believe that."

She smiled slightly. "Thanks. I'm just so ready to be a mother." She felt her eyes welling with tears, but she didn't have time for that. Her morning class started in fifteen minutes, and students would start arriving at any time. "I'd better go. I have a class to teach."

"Okay. I will meet with a new birthmother next week, so hang in there."

"Thanks." She ended the call and sat at her desk, staring out the window in front of her. It overlooked the garden area behind her building, a place she would often sit after classes to get some fresh air and a moment of quiet. She watched a little bird flitting around, going in and out of the nest it was building. She wanted to nest. She wanted to build a life as a wife and mother, and so far she only had the wife part down.

"Hey." She turned around in her swivel chair and saw Tabatha standing there. She quickly wiped away a stray tear and forced a smile.

"Oh, hey. I didn't know you were stopping by this morning."

"I just wanted to bring that book back that you

let me borrow." She reached out her hand and gave it to Janine.

"You already read it?"

"Yes. It answered a lot of questions for me. I had no idea giving birth was going to be so involved. Why did you have that book, anyway?"

"A student gave it to me a while back when I was thinking about..."

"Having a baby?"

She nodded. "Yes. Obviously, that didn't work out. So, now I lend it to my pregnant students."

"Well, thanks. Are you okay?"

"Of course. Why?"

"You looked upset when I came in."

"Oh, I'm fine. Are we still on for our class tomorrow?"

"Yes. I'm looking forward to it."

"Good. I wish I had more time to chat, but my students are coming in. See you tomorrow?"

Tabatha nodded. "See ya."

As she walked out of the studio, Janine worked on gathering herself so she could give her all to her students. She never wanted to give any less than one-hundred percent. No matter what was happening in her personal life, she wouldn't let it affect her job.

Julie walked through the halls of her son's school, holding Dawson's hand. When Mrs. Hamphill had called and asked her to come to the school, her stomach twisted into a million knots. That kind of call was never a good thing.

"What do you think they're going to tell us?"

"I don't know, but we'll figure it all out," Dawson said. His steady demeanor was always her light in the storm. No matter what was happening in their lives, Dawson stayed calm and helped center her. When she would freak out over something, he was there to level her out. They made a great team.

"Mr. and Mrs. Lancaster, I'm so glad you could make it. Come on in." Mrs. Hamphill stepped back and allowed them into the room, shutting the door behind them. "The kids are at extended lunch, so I thought this would be the perfect time to chat. Please, have a seat."

Julie and Dawson sat down in chairs across from her desk. "Thanks for seeing us."

Mrs. Hamphill sat down and looked at them. "I'm afraid I do have some not so good news. It appears Dylan has been getting bullied."

"Bullied? By who?" Julie asked, her anger bubbling up to the surface.

"It's a child in the same grade. They're in PE together. The teacher witnessed it just today, but then he realized he'd seen some signs before."

"Can we have the kid's name?" Dawson asked.

She smiled slightly. "I'm afraid I can't tell you that, but I can coordinate a meeting with the parents with all of us and the school counselor. I've also reported it to the principal, who will talk to the student."

"I can't believe this."

"We have a no tolerance policy for bullying in this district, so rest assured we will put a stop to this. In the meantime, I would encourage you to have a heart to heart talk with Dylan about it."

"We will, of course. But I would like to schedule that meeting." Julie said it through a shaky voice as anger welled inside of her. She was normally a pretty calm person, but anybody bothering her child pulled out a whole different side of her.

"Absolutely. I will text you later today with some dates and times. If you want Dylan to see the counselor, we can also set that up."

"No," Dawson said out of the blue.

"Excuse me?"

"Sorry, I don't mean to be rude. I just don't think Dylan needs to see a counselor. He's a kid. He's a growing boy. He's also tough. We will get him through this as his parents."

"Dawson..." Julie said quietly.

"Please don't think I'm diminishing your role as his parents at all. I just want to provide whatever resources I can."

"And we thank you," Julie said, glancing over at her husband before looking back at the teacher. "I'll look forward to your text."

As they walked back to Dawson's truck, he said nothing. His jaw was tight and twitching, and that wasn't something she'd seen often. He was usually as cool as a cucumber. Once they finally reached his truck, he opened her door, and she climbed inside. He joined her moments later, put his hands on the steering wheel and growled like he'd been holding it in for hours.

"What is going on?"

He sighed and leaned his head back against the seat. "I got bullied when I was his age, and I swore I'd never let that happen to my kid."

She reached over and touched his leg. "You didn't let anything happen, honey. This isn't your fault."

"Maybe I should've toughened him up. Taken

him to karate classes or lifted weights with him. He's short for his age, and he's got that extra weight. I bet they're making jokes about his weight! That's what happened to me…"

"Dawson, take a breath. First of all, you don't need to turn our son into a ninja body builder to protect him. And secondly, we don't even know what this bully is saying or doing. We have to take this one step at a time. Let's go home, have a cup of coffee, and figure out how we're going to talk to Dylan. Okay?"

He looked over at her and smiled. "I'm usually the one calming you down."

"I know. This is weird, and I don't like it one bit."

"I hate this," Celeste said as she got out of the car, carefully holding the top of the door so she didn't fall over. Ben had blindfolded her as soon as they left the house.

"It's romantic."

"It's giving me vertigo. Why did you not only have to blindfold me, but drive in circles to confuse me?"

He laughed. "Because I'm a creative man."

Ben took her hand and led her closer to their destination. She could feel the ocean breeze, but a person could feel that pretty much anywhere in Seagrove. As they walked, she could hear the waves, too. The water was definitely getting closer.

"I feel sand under my shoes," she said, pointing out that she was on to his game. He chuckled.

"Fine, let's take it off."

When Celeste removed the blindfold, her eyes had to adjust a moment in the fading afternoon sunlight. Then, she saw the most beautiful picnic laid out on the beach right next to the lighthouse.

"Oh wow, Ben. This is amazing."

"Really?"

She looked at him. "Really. No one has ever done anything like this for me before. Thank you."

He grinned. "You're welcome. Now, let's eat."

They sat down on the blanket, and Ben started unpacking the picnic basket. He had chicken salad sandwiches, chips and sweet tea from the cafe along with potato salad from her other favorite restaurant. Celeste also recognized SuAnn's famous lemon pound cake.

"These are all my favorite foods from town," she said, looking around.

"I know."

"How did you know I liked all this stuff?"

He smiled sheepishly. "Well, you told me about the pound cake. Abigail helped me with the chicken salad, and I asked around at a couple of restaurants I knew you'd been to before."

She struggled to hold back tears, which was a surprise to her. In her whole life of bouncing around the foster care system and then struggling as an adult, no one had ever done anything even close to this for her. For the first time in her life, she felt cared for, respected, and wanted. It was almost overwhelming.

"Ben… this… is…"

He stopped what he was doing and leaned over, taking one of her hands in his. "Are you okay?"

She felt her body start to shudder and then tears started to fall, even though she tried with all her might to stop them. "Dang it! I hate crying!"

He stifled a laugh. "I can see that. You look like you're going to explode."

Celeste chuckled and wiped her eyes with the back of her sleeve. "I'm sorry. I must look like a crazy person. Who cries over a picnic?"

He looked into her eyes. "Someone who's never had a person do this for them?"

"Sad, huh?"

"Celeste, you didn't cause what happened to you while you were growing up. It makes me mad and sad every time I let myself think about what you went through. I'm honored to get to be the person who shows you how amazing you are."

"Stop! I'm going to cry again."

"You deserve all the good things."

"Thank you."

"Now, let's eat. I'm starving!"

"Me too. I do have one question, though."

"What's that?" he asked, as he put straws into the cups of sweet tea.

"How many women have you done this for?"

"A picnic?"

"Yes."

"Just you."

"Oh, come on. You won't hurt my feelings if you tell the truth."

"Seriously, just you. I chose this because I thought it'd be cool if we both had our first picnic together."

Celeste had never been sure what people meant when they said their heart skipped a beat, or they had butterflies in their stomach until right now. It felt like a party in the middle of her body, and it both scared her and made her happier than she'd ever been in her life.

Janine picked at her sandwich and stared out over the town square. She tried not to focus on the happy mothers wheeling their babies around in strollers or the adorable toddlers running across the grassy area.

"Earth to Janine," William said, waving his hand in front of her face.

She looked back at him. "Sorry. I guess I was lost in thought for a minute."

"I see them too, you know."

She smiled sadly. "I don't know why this is getting to me so bad. I mean, I've gone without children for all my life, and now my biological clock suddenly kicks into gear?"

He laughed. "We have the rest of our lives in front of us, Janine. There's no need to rush. When God means for us to adopt a child, the right situation will appear."

"Funny you should say that, because I feel like God is teasing me."

"What do you mean?"

She took a bite of her sandwich and paused for a

moment. "You know I'm giving Tabatha private classes, right?"

"Yeah."

"Well, I feel like she's leaning toward giving her baby up for adoption, and there's a part of me that ached to ask her if we could adopt her child. How horrible of a person am I?"

"That's not horrible, Janine. You want to give her baby a wonderful home. Maybe she'd be open to it."

"Absolutely not! I would never want her to feel pressured by anyone. I just needed to admit my horrible thoughts out loud."

He reached across the table and squeezed her hand. "Honey, it will happen. Somebody will pick us."

"And what if they don't?"

"Then I'll wait here until I see an exhausted mother with a crying baby and see if she wants a break for about eighteen years."

"William!" she said, slapping his hand. "You're awful."

Julie was a nervous wreck as she and Dawson waited for Dylan to get off the bus. They'd decided to sit down with him and talk about the bullying before he had the chance to disappear to his room until dinner.

"I hate having conversations like this," she said, fidgeting in her seat on the sofa. "I feel like we're having an intervention."

Dawson laughed. "Let's be glad that's not the case."

Before Julie could respond, she heard the bus stopping outside. Moments later, Dylan walked through the door, hung his backpack on the peg by the door, and then noticed his parents sitting on the sofa.

"What's going on?"

"We wanted to talk to you about something," Dawson said, pointing for him to sit in the chair across from the sofa.

"Now? I was going to eat something and play video games."

"We won't keep you long, Dylan," Julie said, staring at him for a moment longer until he sat down.

"Ugh," he said, sighing. "What did I do?"

"You did nothing wrong, son," Dawson said. "But I need you to be honest with me about something, okay?"

"Okay."

"Are you getting bullied at school?"

Dylan's eyes widened. "Who told you that?"

"Mrs. Hamphill. We met with her, and she spoke to some of your other teachers as well," Julie said, her tone sympathetic.

"Oh, my gosh! Y'all are going to get me killed!" Dylan said, standing up and stomping his foot.

"Calm down, Dylan. We're just trying to help..." Dawson said, holding up his hand.

"Help? It's bad enough I get picked on, but when the kids find out my mom and dad came to the school... It's going to be awful now!"

"Sit down," Dawson said, firmly.

Dylan sat back down, his arms crossed and his bottom lip poked out well beyond where it normally was. His eyebrows were furrowed together so tightly that Julie figured she couldn't get a piece of thread between them.

"Honey, you've been very different these last few weeks since going back to school after winter break. We couldn't get you to tell us what was wrong, so we thought maybe your teachers could shed some light. It's only because we love you that we wanted to find out how we could help you. We never dreamed you were being bullied."

"Everybody gets bullied at some point. It's just my turn," he mumbled.

"No, it's not your turn. You don't deserve to be bullied, Dylan."

"What they're saying is true, though."

"What?"

"One of the kids found out about my mother and foster care. They keep making jokes about me being an orphan and how nobody wanted me."

Julie felt like her head was going to explode. She'd never felt such anger in her life, even when her ex-husband had cheated and had a baby with another woman. This kind of anger, about her child, was next level.

"Those aren't jokes. That is just meanness. Your mother loves you even now, Dylan. You know that. And your father loved you, too. And we love you. You've been wanted by every person who has known you," she said.

"Do we have to keep talking about this?" he groaned, hanging his head.

"We want to help you, son. We won't allow this to continue to go on. Now, who is the boy bullying you? What's his name?" Dawson asked.

Dylan looked at him like he had two heads. "What?"

"I want to know who this boy is so I can have a chat with his father."

He paused for a long moment and then looked down at his hands. "Dad, it isn't a boy."

Dawson cleared his throat and shifted uncomfortably in his seat. "It's not a boy?"

"That's what he said, sweetie," Julie said, giving him a stern look. "Bullying isn't just reserved for boys. Girls can be bullies too."

"Her name's Jacie. I had a crush on her, and one of my friends told her friend. She got embarrassed and started saying mean things. Then other people said mean things."

Julie stood up and crouched beside his chair, her hand on his knee. "The school is having a talk with her and her parents, and we'll be having a meeting with them as well. This won't continue happening, Dylan."

He stood up abruptly and stomped his foot. "Why did you have to go over there? It's bad enough to be bullied, but to have my parents go to the school and embarrass me is way worse!"

"Dylan..." Julie said, standing up.

"Leave me alone!" He stomped up the stairs and slammed his bedroom door, something Julie and Dawson had never seen him do before.

"Well, that could've gone way better," Julie said, sitting back down on the sofa.

"It's because she's a girl."

"What?"

"Boys are used to being bullied by other boys. It's a part of life for most of us, unless you're the 'top dog', so to speak. But for the girl he likes to make fun of him that way? Not good. His ego is bruised, and his feelings are hurt."

"I don't blame him. What kind of parents raise a kid who would say such things?"

"We're going to find out soon enough."

She looked at him, anger on her face. "Yes, we are."

CHAPTER 5

ABIGAIL FRANTICALLY JUMPED OUT OF THE CAR, THE night air nipping at her uncovered arms. She'd forgotten to change out of her t-shirt and flannel pajama pants before racing toward the vet clinic.

She opened the passenger door and retrieved Petunia, who was restless and had been vomiting for the last hour. Without thinking, she'd put her in the car and zipped across town, all without even calling the doctor first. Her puppy needed help, and she was determined to save her life.

She held Petunia in one hand and pounded on the door of the clinic with the other. Realizing it was after nine o'clock and Griffin wouldn't still be there, she ran around the side of the building and toward the house where he lived. She banged on that door, noticing the flicker of a TV in the window.

Griffin opened the door, his eyes wide. He was wearing a gray t-shirt and jeans, and holding the TV remote. "Abigail? What's going on?"

"Petunia ate chocolate!" Before getting a puppy, Abigail had read many websites about how to care for a puppy, and she knew chocolate could be toxic to dogs. Even though she was very careful about leaving stuff like that lying around, Tabatha wasn't. A pregnant woman sometimes needed chocolate, and she wouldn't begrudge her that, but somehow Petunia had found it, and now Abigail was terrified she was going to die.

"Okay, let's go over to the clinic," he said, grabbing the keys off a hook near his front door. He jogged across the small area of lawn that separated his home from the office and quickly opened the door. By now, Petunia was more lethargic. She didn't even react with a tail wag when she saw Griffin. "Put her on the table."

Abigail carefully laid her down, feeling more out of control than she ever had. "I guess you should've adopted her after all. She would've been safer with you," she said, holding back tears.

"Don't say that. Accidents happen all the time. Now, how much did she eat?"

"I'm not really sure. It wasn't mine. I don't even like chocolate."

He stopped what he was doing and looked at her. "You don't like chocolate? I'm busy right now, but we need to come back to that."

"Anyway, there's a pregnant woman staying with us, and I think it was hers. She must have dropped a bar on the floor and not realized it."

"If Petunia ate a whole bar of chocolate at her size, we need to take action. Has she been vomiting or had diarrhea?"

"Vomiting for about an hour."

"Her breathing is a bit rapid, too. Do you know what kind of chocolate she ate? Or when?"

"No idea what type, but I think Tabatha eats mainly dark chocolate. And it was about an hour and a half ago… I think."

"I'm going to give her a shot to help her vomit more."

"More? Why?"

"If any is left in her stomach, we need to get it out. I'll also give her fluids at the same time so she doesn't dehydrate. Then I'll give her activated charcoal to remove the toxin from her body."

"Is she going to be okay?"

He looked at her. "I can't promise anything until we see how she reacts. If you want to go home, I'll take good care of her overnight."

Abigail shook her head. "I'm not leaving her."

Griffin paused for a moment. "Okay, but why don't you go sit down over there for a bit? I need some space."

Abigail realized she'd been hovering over the table, almost elbowing him out of the way, and that wasn't a good thing for Petunia. She turned and went to sit in the waiting area, her eyes focused on what he was doing. It was amazing how quickly she'd fallen in love with her puppy.

After a few minutes, he had her hooked up to fluids and had given her the shot for vomiting. Thankfully, it didn't seem like she had a lot left in her system. Abigail sat there, praying that Petunia made it. Finally, she seemed to fall asleep and Griffin walked over.

"I think she's going to be okay, but I need to keep her on fluids and activated charcoal overnight. Once she seems back to her peppy self, you can take her home. Are you sure you want to stay here? I promise to call if anything changes."

Abigail shook her head. "I'm staying."

"You know, I don't normally let owners stay in my waiting room all night."

"I took karate as a kid, and I'm not afraid to use it, Griffin."

He laughed. "I don't want to get kicked, so I guess I'll let you crash here. These chairs aren't exactly comfortable," he said, sitting down.

"No, they really aren't. They look like they were manufactured before I was born."

"They probably were. Papa Doc was a frugal man."

"Were you really close to him?"

"Yeah. I adored that man. He was everything I want to be, minus the bad taste in decor, of course. Did you have grandparents you were close to?"

"No. I grew up in foster care, actually."

There was a long pause. "I'm sorry."

Abigail smiled. "It's okay. It wasn't so bad. I was lucky compared to a lot of kids."

"So, how did you end up in Seagrove?"

"After my dad died, I was in foster care and got placed here with a woman named Elaine Benson. I was in her home for a couple of years before getting adopted by a couple in Tennessee."

"And you're back in Seagrove?"

"Kind of a long story, but Elaine left her house to me and another foster kid."

"Wow! She must've really loved you."

"Yeah. I loved her too."

"I have this secret fear that I'll run my grandfather's business into the ground. He worked so hard for many years, and I don't want to wreck it."

"I'm sure you'll do great."

Griffin chuckled. "Is this from the same woman who yelled at me at the animal shelter?"

"I didn't yell. And you called me a kidnapper!"

He shrugged his shoulders. "I wanted Petunia really bad."

"What about Bingo?"

He smiled. "I adore that dog. He's amazing. In fact, he's in my bed right now."

"Well, you might've gotten the better end of that deal. Petunia, as it turns out, is a handful."

He stood up and walked over to the puppy to check on her. After a few moments, he returned to his seat. "She's resting comfortably right now. Respiration is looking better."

"Good."

"You really can go home, Abigail. I'll take good care of her. I know you don't trust me just yet..."

"I actually do trust you. I don't know why, but

I do."

He smiled slightly. "Thanks."

"So, where did you grow up?"

"My first ten years or so were in Charleston. Then my parents divorced, and my mom took us to Tennessee."

"And your dad?"

"He moved to Oklahoma, started a new family and never looked back."

"Oh wow. That had to be tough."

"It was. A boy needs his father. I was close to my dad, or so I thought. I heard he had twin boys and then a little girl. Once I turned thirteen or so, I never heard from him again."

"Is your mom still around?"

He laughed. "My mom was a bit of a free spirit. When I was in high school, she started studying energy healing and astrology. Once I went off to college, she joined some commune in Bali and lived there for many years. Unfortunately, she passed away of cancer about three years ago. She once told me that energy never dies. It just changes forms, so she's still around me in some way."

"She sounds like she was an interesting lady." Petunia groaned, and he went to check on her again. "Is she okay?"

"I think she's perking up a bit. Listen, I can give her fluids at my house, and we can all be more comfortable. Maybe make a pot of coffee?"

She hesitated for a moment. Go to a strange man's house for the night? It probably wasn't her best idea, but she would not leave Petunia until she knew she was all right. If she went home, she'd just be up all night worrying anyway.

"Okay, but let me text my roommate, Celeste, and let her know what's going on. I ran out of the house so fast that she's probably getting worried." In all likelihood, Celeste was asleep and had no idea she was gone, but it made her feel better to let someone know where she was.

Celeste felt somebody tapping her on the shoulder repeatedly, and her first thought was to punch them square in the jaw, roll over and go back to sleep. She opened one eye and looked at the clock on her nightstand. It was two o'clock in the morning, and this had better be good.

"What?" she groaned, without bothering to open both of her eyes.

"Celeste, I think I'm in labor!" Tabatha yelped

between her own groans.

Celeste immediately sat up in her bed, flipped on her lamp, and saw Tabatha holding her stomach.

"Did your water break?"

"No, but I've got these pains worse than cramps."

She got out of bed and put on her shoes, thankful that she'd fallen asleep wearing a sweatshirt and yoga pants the night before. "Let me put my hair up, and we'll head to the hospital."

Tabatha carefully walked down the stairs and sat on the bench by the front door to wait. Celeste ran down the hallway, calling for Abigail before finally looking at her phone. She was at the vet with her sick puppy and wouldn't be home until morning. Knowing what time it was, she opted not to text Abigail and just handle this on her own.

"Everything okay?"

Celeste was startled when she saw Ben come out of his office. "What on earth are you doing here at this hour?"

"I couldn't sleep, so I came to do paperwork around midnight. I didn't want to wake you. Is everything okay?"

"Tabatha is having contractions."

His eyes widened. "Isn't it a little early?"

"Yes. Plus the fact that she hasn't made a decision," Celeste whispered.

"You know I can hear y'all, right?"

Celeste cleared her throat. "Sorry. Let's go."

"I'm coming with you," Ben said, shutting the door to his office.

Ten minutes later, they pulled up to the ER. Celeste was thankful it was close because she didn't want to help Tabatha give birth to a baby in her car. She'd never really wanted to be a mother, and giving birth freaked her out.

"Let me help you," Ben said, holding Tabatha's hand as he eased her out of the car. He walked her through the double doors that opened into the emergency room. She held her stomach, occasionally making a groaning noise. Celeste followed closely behind them, leaving her car at the door. She figured Ben could move it to the parking lot for her after they got Tabatha checked in.

"Can I help you folks?" an amiable woman with a thick southern accent asked as they approached the desk.

"This is Tabatha, and she thinks she might be in labor."

The woman looked at Tabatha, surprise on her face for just a moment before she looked down at her computer. It was obvious to Celeste that the woman was shocked by Tabatha's age. Not only was she sixteen years old, but she was a young looking sixteen. If Celeste didn't know her, she would've mistaken her for twelve or thirteen, at most.

"Okay, hon, let me get you a wristband and we'll bring you back to triage."

"What's triage?" Tabatha asked.

The woman smiled. "Triage is just where they take your blood pressure and other vitals."

Tabatha nodded. "Can I sit down?"

"Of course. Here's your wristband," she said, quickly wrapping it around Tabatha's wrist. Celeste helped her over to one of the chairs and eased her down into it.

Tabatha wasn't a tall girl. She was probably no more than five-foot-two, and being this pregnant made her look incredibly uncomfortable. Celeste was happy she had never had to go through pregnancy, although sometimes she did think about her older years and who might take care of her.

Not having any family presented its own set of challenges and problems, but she tried not to think about them because there wasn't much she could do. Even if she got married, there was no guarantee that her husband would outlive her, so she had to think about things like long-term care insurance and possible nursing home facilities for herself, both pretty depressing trains of thought.

Why these types of thoughts were floating through her head in the middle of an emergency room was beyond her. Sometimes she just pondered the future, and it seemed a little bleak. Not necessarily because she wanted children, but because she just wanted to be surrounded by people who actually cared about her, whoever they were.

The last few months in Seagrove had given her the hope that maybe she could find something like that. Maybe she could have a family that wasn't blood related, but cared about her more than her blood family did in the first place.

Maybe there was hope that people would love her, and take care of her, just because of who she was. Maybe she didn't have to have her own children to feel safe and protected as she got older or when she needed someone.

“I’m going to go move the car," Ben said, without her having to ask him. It was nice that he just knew to go do that without her saying a word.

"Are you in a lot of pain?"

"Yeah, it hurts every few minutes. I guess that's contractions?"

"It's still a little early, so maybe it's just something

else. I'm not exactly experienced when it comes to labor and delivery," Celeste said, laughing.

"Did you call Abigail?"

"No. It seems she had an emergency with Petunia and had to go to the after hours vet. I didn't want to stress her out, so I'll talk to her when the sun comes up."

"Probably a good idea. There's nothing she can really do for me right now, anyway."

"You know, it's going to be okay. The doctors know exactly what to do, so I know you and the baby will be fine."

Tabatha nodded, her eyes welling with tears a bit. "It sucks not having a family."

Celeste nodded. "I know what you mean. Even if we have family that isn't that great, you still want them there. You still want people to care about you and have your back. But I want you to know that we aren't your blood family, but we have your back, Tabatha. We won't let anything happen to you."

She leaned over and laid her head on Celeste's shoulder, something she had never done before. For a moment, Celeste got a taste of that maternal instinct, wanting to stand up and put a high fence around Tabatha. Unfortunately, the world had a way of knocking down those fences, anyway.

Ben walked back into the emergency room and sat down beside Celeste. "Have they taken her back for vitals yet?"

"Not yet."

He stood up and walked to the front desk. "Excuse me? This young woman is in terrible pain, and it seems to me that your waiting area is completely empty. I'm Dr. Ben Callaway, a pediatrician in Seagrove. I would hate to think that anything happens to her or her baby because of inadequate healthcare."

Celeste could not believe what she was hearing. Ben was the most laid-back guy she had ever met, and he was making a scene. She didn't know whether to be irritated or impressed.

"I'm sorry, sir. We had a car accident come in about thirty minutes ago, and it's all hands on deck. I've placed a call to our OB/GYN, and she's on her way in right now."

He nodded his head. "Thank you."

He walked back over and sat down next to Celeste as if nothing had ever happened.

"What was all that about?" she whispered to him.

He smiled, slyly. "Was I impressive?"

"Maybe a little," she said, chuckling.

In another minute, the nurse called Tabatha to

the back. Was it because Ben made his little speech? She didn't know, but he looked pretty proud of himself.

"Can I go with her?" Celeste asked, standing up.

"I'm just taking her vitals, and then I'll send her right back out."

"Okay." Celeste slowly sat back down, watching as Tabatha disappeared into a small room, the door shutting behind her.

"You really care about her, don't you?"

She sighed. "More than I've cared about a teenager in my life."

"She's going to be fine. I've been watching her, and I think she's having Braxton Hicks contractions."

"You mean like false labor?"

"Yes. I've been timing her grimaces, and they aren't close together or regular."

She smiled. "I guess it's good to have a doctor in the family." As soon as she said it, she wanted to reel it back inside her body.

"In the family?"

"You know what I mean."

He smiled and leaned back. "I'm not sure I do, but I'll take it."

CHAPTER 6

The early morning sunlight peeked through the blinds, temporarily blinding Abigail as she slowly opened her eyes. There are those moments in the morning where a person forgets where they are for a moment as they try to reconnect to reality.

She eased herself up, realizing she was lying on an unfamiliar surface. It took her a moment to remember that she was at Griffin's house, and she had slept on the sofa. She remembered Griffin offering to give up his bed, but there was no way she was doing that. Besides, his sofa was quite plush and comfortable.

"Good morning. How'd you sleep?" She turned to see him standing in the kitchen, his hair slightly messy, wearing a pair of plaid pajama pants and a light gray T-shirt that hugged his body in all the right places. How had she not noticed he was so muscular? Was he one of those guys who spent all of his time in the gym?

"Surprisingly well. You should rent out your sofa. I think you could get good money for it."

He laughed. "Coffee?"

"Yes, please." She stood up and slowly walked over to the breakfast bar, sitting down on a stool. "Have you checked on Petunia this morning?"

"I've been checking on Miss Petunia all night. She's doing really well. I think she's pretty much back to her normal self."

"Thank goodness. I was so scared last night. I guess I should've taken her to the emergency vet, but I didn't even think about it. I just came straight here."

He smiled, sliding a cup of coffee across the bar along with a carton of creamer and a bowl of sugar.

"No problem. In a small town, I expect things like that. I want people to trust me with their animals."

"You're a good vet. I'll give you that."

"I consider that high praise coming from you."

She laughed. "I know I seem a little uptight and maybe rude, but I'm not normally that way. I've been under a lot of stress lately, and I might've taken a bit of it out on you."

"I understand. Stress is a killer, so we all have to find ways to deal with it better."

"I'm going to start some yoga classes soon."

He chuckled. "Nothing against yoga, but I happen to think that farm work is the best type of exercise."

She furrowed her eyebrows. "Farm work? So you think I need to come over here and toss around some bales of hay?"

"Sounds like a great idea to me! I had a little farm back in Nashville, and now I have this one. It keeps you in good shape. You get to be close to nature, and you don't have a lot of time to think about your problems."

"Are you telling me you don't go to the gym?"

He looked down at his shirt and then flexed his biceps. "These are all farm grown."

Abigail rolled her eyes and took a sip of her coffee. "I think I'm going to go check on Petunia."

She walked down the hallway into the spare bedroom where Petunia had slept. The puppy went crazy as soon as she walked in the room, jumping up and down behind the small enclosure that Griffin had set up.

"Petunia!" Abigail squealed, running over and then dropping to her knees next to the fencing. She gave her a kiss as Petunia licked her face a million times. Griffin laughed.

"You can pick her up. In fact, I think I will approve her release from this facility."

She picked a very wiggly Petunia up. "What do I owe you?"

He waved his hand. "Nothing."

"I can't pay you nothing, Griffin. You spent all night with her."

"So did you."

"Still, I wouldn't feel right."

"Do you cook?"

"What?"

"Do you cook? You know, like food?"

"Somewhat."

"Sounds promising," he said, laughing. "Okay, what about this? For payment, you bring the ingredients here, and I'll cook."

"How is that payment?" she asked, laughing.

"I'm lonely here in a new town, and I'd like to share a home cooked meal with someone. You'd be helping me out."

She eyed him carefully. "So if I buy the ingredients, and let you cook dinner for me, then we're square? That sounds like a terrible deal for you, but I'd be foolish not to agree to those terms."

Griffin smiled. “I’ll text you the ingredient list. How about tomorrow night?”

“Sounds good.” Abigail squeezed Petunia tightly, being careful not to hurt her. "You're right, she is totally back to herself. I'm so relieved!"

"I think she's going to have a long, happy life as long as you keep the chocolate away from her."

"Don't worry. I'll be having a talk with everybody in my house about that very subject. Speaking of that, I should probably get home. I'm sure Celeste and Tabatha are worried, probably not about me, but more about the puppy."

Griffin smiled. "Well, I know it wasn't what you had planned last night, but I enjoyed hanging out with you, Abigail. I’m glad we get to do it again."

Suddenly, she felt a swarm of butterflies bouncing around in her stomach. What was he saying, exactly? Was he just being polite, veterinarian to customer? Or was he saying that he wanted to spend more time with her as friends? On a date? Was this dinner he was planning actually a date?

As usual, she was overthinking things. Right now, she needed to focus on getting her puppy home and getting back into her routine. Plus, she was thinking about taking a nice, long nap.

"It was nice getting to know you as well. I will recommend your services to everybody I meet."

"Thanks," he said, smiling.

He walked her to the door. "Thanks again for everything."

"You're welcome, Abigail. And you be a good girl, Petunia," he said, petting the top of her head. "Oh, and let's leave Petunia at home when you come to dinner, because I plan to have chocolate around here. We don't want a repeat of this scenario."

"Absolutely." Abigail turned and walked out to her car, putting Petunia in the passenger seat before sliding into the driver side.

As she drove away, she could see Griffin in her rearview mirror, his hand raised in the air, waving goodbye. For some reason, she felt a pit in her stomach, like she didn't want to go home. She wanted to stay there and hang out with him for the rest of the day. Or maybe the rest of the week? All she knew was that the feeling made her very uncomfortable.

Janine unlocked the door to the yoga studio and walked inside, locking it behind her. Her first class wasn't for another hour, but she liked to get there early, so she was ready for the day. The first thing she always did, after turning on the lights, was get the tea cart ready.

There was no question that tea was an important part of yoga for most students. She had a wide selection, and she loved sharing it with them.

Then she walked into the office, opened the computer, and started reading emails. This morning, she was surprised to see an email from the social worker. It was a simple email, just asking her to call when she got a chance.

Janine noticed that the email was sent at three o'clock in the morning, which was an odd thing. Why would the social worker be emailing her at that hour?

She picked up the phone and dialed the number, all the while going through the rest of her emails and deleting what she didn't need.

"Hi, this is Janine. I got your email."

"Janine, I'm so glad you called me!"

"I was surprised to see that you emailed me at three o'clock in the morning. You must be quite a night owl."

She laughed. "It was a bit of an unusual situation. Last night, I was contacted by another social worker who has a birth mother who will be giving birth any day now. She has chosen you and your husband."

Janine froze. She felt like her breath wouldn't move. It was just stuck somewhere in her chest, like a big ball of yarn that needed to be untangled.

"What?"

"I know this is surprising, and you may not be quite ready, but she really would like for you and your husband to raise her child. She should have the baby by the end of the week. If you don't feel like you can handle this..."

"No! Of course we can handle this! I guess I'm just shocked. I can't wait to tell William!"

"I'm going to email you some information because this is going to be quite a quick process. Be on the lookout for that, and you might want to start getting that nursery ready!"

As Janine hung up the phone, she couldn't believe what had just happened. She sat there for a moment, staring off into space, before she felt the tears flowing from her eyes. She was finally going to be a mother. She'd waited her whole life for this, and she had to go tell her husband.

She quickly texted him to ask where he was, assuming he was out on the boat. Turned out, he was just next door at the bakery having breakfast with his mom. Now she would be able to tell both of them at the same time. Then she would run down to the bookstore and tell her sister before it was time to teach her first class.

Janine didn't know how she was going to keep it together during class. The excitement was already overwhelming her, and she wasn't sure if she'd be able to wipe the smile off her face.

She grabbed her keys, ran out the front door, and locked it behind her. She walked quickly next door to Hotcakes and walked in to see William sitting with his mother having danish and coffee. SuAnn was standing behind the counter working with other customers. Janine gave her a quick wave and then sat down with her husband and mother-in-law. SuAnn was busy serving customers, so Janine would tell her what was going on after she was finished.

"Hey, honey. I thought you had a class to teach?" William said.

"I do. But not for another hour. Listen, it's good that you're both here because I need to talk to you about something.

“You sure you want me here?” Dixie asked.

"Of course. This is life-changing information." Janine couldn't help but sit there with a big grin on her face. She probably looked like a crazy person.

"So, what is this big news?" William asked.

"The social worker just called. A birth mother chose us, and she will have the baby any day now!"

William's eyes widened and looked almost as big as saucers. "Are you serious?"

"I'm serious!"

Dixie clapped her hands and let out a big laugh. "Well, this calls for a celebration! SuAnn, bring us a round of your best peach cobbler!"

SuAnn looked at them like they were all nuts. "What on earth is going on over there?"

"Never you mind! Just bring us the cobbler!" Dixie called back. The two of them had become good friends, but they were always picking at each other and making sarcastic comments. Janine loved it.

"So we're going to have a baby within the week?"

Janine nodded her head, smiling. "It appears so. I don't even know the gender. I didn't ask. But we do need to start shopping for nursery stuff. There's so much to do!"

"Don't worry. I'll help however I can. I can't believe I'm going to be a grandma! What should the baby call me?"

"Granny?" William offered.

"Honey, I'm not granny yet. I don't sit in rocking

chairs or wear my hair in a bun. I don't put my glasses down at the tip of my nose either."

William laughed. "Oh, are those the criteria for being called granny?"

"I need something snazzier. I'll have to think about that."

He rolled his eyes. "Well, you work on that while we work on getting this baby home. What can I do?"

"Start clearing out the guest room?"

He looked at his watch. "I have a tour this morning, but as soon as I get home after lunch, I'll start doing that."

She smiled. "We're getting a baby. We're about to be parents."

"I know, and I'm scared to death."

Dixie reached across the table, taking each of their hands. "Listen, you two. You're going to be wonderful parents. There isn't a handbook, and none of us knew what the heck we were doing in the beginning. It's the love that matters. The love is what will guide every decision you make for your child. When the love is strong, you'll do right by your child every time."

SuAnn walked over and set three plates of peach cobbler on the table. "Now, what's with all the yelling over here?"

Janine smiled at her. "You're going to be a grandma again!"

"I can't believe it was false labor," Tabatha said, sighing as she walked into the house.

"It happens a lot. No need to feel bad about it," Ben said. He unlocked the door to his office, ready to start seeing patients for the day. He'd had to call several patients to push their appointments back slightly.

"I'm just ready to not be pregnant anymore."

"Where have y'all been?" Abigail asked as she came out of the kitchen.

"We were at the hospital all night," Celeste said, hanging her backpack on the hook by the front door. She hated to carry a regular purse, but a backpack wasn't a problem.

"Oh, my gosh! At the hospital? Is everything okay?"

"It was just false labor," Tabatha said, hanging her head. "I think I'm going to go upstairs and take a nap."

Without another word, she went up the stairs,

leaving Abigail, Celeste, and Ben standing in the foyer.

"Why didn't you text me?" Abigail asked.

"Because you were dealing with the puppy, and there was nothing you could do. I was just going to wait until morning, but then they sent her home."

"Is anybody else worried that she hasn't made a decision yet?" Abigail asked.

"Yeah. Things are getting all too real. I'm ready to support her on whatever she chooses, but she's got to make a choice soon. There are things that need to happen between now and the time that baby gets here."

Abigail nodded. "Yeah. If she's going to pursue adoption, she needs to start looking at adoptive parents. If she's going to keep the baby, she's got to work out living arrangements, a crib, a stroller…"

Celeste held up her hand. "Listen, I know all of that. I'm exhausted. I was up all night with her, so I think I'm going to take a nap too while I have a chance. Is the puppy okay?"

"She's fine. But nobody is to have chocolate in this house anytime soon," Abigail said.

"I'm not sure exactly what that means, but we can fight about it later," Celeste said as she walked up the stairs toward her room.

Julie could hardly contain herself. Janine and William were going to be parents, and it could be any day now. She was so excited about their good fortune, and she was also thrilled for the baby who would get them as parents.

"I can't help being excited for my sister, but I'm also nervous about this meeting." She and Dawson had just arrived at the school to meet with the parents of Jacie, the bully. Dylan had no idea they were there, and they hoped they didn't run into him in the hallway. He was going to be upset when he found out about this meeting actually happening.

"I'm excited for them too, but I'm really focused on this meeting. I feel like things could get out of hand really quickly if these parents don't take accountability."

"We just need to keep our cool as much as possible."

They got out of the car and walked down the hallway to the counselor's office. When they opened the door, they saw another couple, the counselor and one of Dylan's teachers.

"Mr. and Mrs. Lancaster, we're happy to have you. Please, everyone, follow me into the conference room," Mr. Rollins, the counselor, said. The couple didn't look happy, and she thought it was weird that no one introduced themselves. With no words exchanged, both sets of parents followed him and sat down.

"I know this is an unusual situation, and it's certainly not something anyone relishes talking about. Bullying is not tolerated in our school system, but it's been brought to my attention that this might not be a simple case of bullying."

"Because she's a girl? You don't think girls can be bullies to boys?" Julie blurted out. Dawson squeezed her hand, trying to warn her to calm down.

"Of course we don't think that, Mrs. Lancaster. "

"Please call me Julie."

"Okay. It doesn't matter if it's a boy or a girl doing the bullying. However, it seems that there is some additional history between these kids that you don't know about."

"And what is that? I know that my son had a crush on your daughter, and she didn't like that, so she said some very nasty things about him being adopted. What more could there be?"

The woman, whose name Julie still didn't know, glared at her. "The truth is that your son would not leave my daughter alone. He kept putting notes in her locker, making posters, asking her to go on a picnic with him, and even showed up at our house one day and knocked on the front door. You obviously haven't taught him the meaning of the word no."

Julie was stunned. "School crushes are pretty common. And I have a son who is extremely respectful, so I don't believe he did anything out of the ordinary. Have you ever experienced young love?"

The woman crossed her arms and pursed her lips. "When a young woman says she's not interested, then a young man should be respectful enough to leave her alone."

"Excuse me, but you're acting like he was stalking her. He's a little boy! He had a crush, and he thought she might be interested in him. Instead, she was hateful. I can only imagine what kind of parents would raise someone to say such ugly things!"

"Ladies! Let's not allow this to descend into an argument. We are trying to teach our children how to be respectful of each other, so let's try to do the same," Mr. Rollins said. Both women sat back, arms crossed, and refused to look at each other. Julie didn't care if it was immature. Right now, she was just trying not to lunge across the room.

"So what are you proposing, Mr. Rollins?" Dawson asked.

"I think each of you needs to talk to your children. Jacie needs to be told that it's never okay to bully someone, even with your words. And Dylan needs to understand that when a young woman says she's not interested, he has to take her at her word."

"And you're just believing what these people are telling you? We know for certain that Jacie bullied our son. Do you have proof that he did the things she's accusing him of? Because that doesn't sound like my son. He's quiet and shy, and if she wasn't interested, he wouldn't have continued on."

"Maybe you need to talk to your son about boundaries," the woman said, sticking her nose in the air. Julie felt like reaching across and pinching it off.

She could truly see why Jacie was the way she was. Her parents didn't want to take any accountability, and the mother, at the very least, seemed the epitome of snooty. The father, on the other hand, wouldn't make eye contact with anybody and never said a word. Julie wondered if he was able to speak. Living with that woman was probably part of the problem. The man probably lived in fear of giving his opinion.

"I think we need to have another meeting with the children present," Mr. Rollins said.

"What? That doesn't seem very wise to me," Julie said.

"These kids need to learn how to handle conflict appropriately. It seems their parents aren't teaching them that," Mr. Rollins said. Now Julie wanted to smack him, too.

"Fine. Why don't we bring the kids down here? They're both in class right now, so why wait?" Julie said.

"If everybody can hang around for another half hour, we will let the kids miss PE class, and we will have a conversation. And then I will talk about any disciplinary actions that need to happen."

Everybody nodded, and nobody looked at each other. The anger in the room was palpable, and Julie was worried about how her son was going to react when he walked into a room full of adults who were mad at each other.

CHAPTER 7

"GOOD MORNING, AGAIN," BEN SAID, SMILING AS Celeste appeared in the kitchen. It was just around nine o'clock, so she was surprised to see him standing there, wearing an apron and cooking scrambled eggs.

"What are you doing? I thought you had some patients?"

"I did. I have a little break before my next one, so I thought I would cook you and Tabatha some breakfast. I couldn't find real bacon, so I have some turkey bacon in the microwave."

"Thank you," she said, sitting down at the bar. He poured her a cup of coffee and slid it over to her. Celeste liked to drink her coffee black, which was no surprise, given that she had worked on so many construction sites throughout her life. Construction workers tended to drink their coffee black too, so she would rarely see anybody putting sugar or creamer into their cup. It was almost sacrilegious.

"Is Tabatha still asleep?"

"I think so. I didn't want to open her door and wake her up. She had a very long night, as you well know."

"I really hate that this is how she's spending her time as a teenager."

"Me too. Although I understand what it's like to miss out on things during your high school years. I never even went to prom."

"Really? Why not?"

Celeste laughed. "Well, when you're taller than pretty much any boy in your school, and most of them are afraid of you anyway, you don't get invitations to school dances."

"Models are tall."

"Yes, but I was tall *and* mean. I didn't exactly exude positivity or welcomeness."

"You were going through a lot of stuff back then as a foster kid. I'm sure nobody blamed you for feeling the way you did."

He slid a plate in front of her and handed her a fork. Celeste took a bite, happy to have some food in her stomach that didn't come from a hospital vending machine.

"I can look back on it now and forgive myself for wasting the opportunity to make friends and have experiences. At the time, I didn't think I wanted either of those things. I hated everybody, honestly. The more I ease into my life here, the more I see what I missed out on."

"We all have regrets like that, I'm sure."

"Tabatha won't get to go to her prom because she'll either be dealing with a new baby or the fallout that will come along with giving her baby to someone else. Her high school experience won't be what it could've been because of what that boy did to her."

"I heard that he's been charged for what he did?"

"That's my understanding, but she doesn't like to talk about it. When she has to go testify, it's going to be very difficult for her."

"She's a senior next year, right?"

"Yes."

"Maybe she can go to prom then."

Celeste laughed. "I think prom is really the least of her worries right now. I know I'm not her mother, but I feel like I need to have a talk with her about making a decision. The reality is that the baby could come at any moment, and she's not prepared at all. It's like she's frozen and unable to decide. Somebody has to give her an ultimatum of sorts."

"Give who an ultimatum?"

They turned to see Tabatha standing in the doorway, sleep still in her eyes. She was wearing a pair of maternity pajamas and a ratty old bathrobe that Celeste had found in one of the closets.

"I didn't see you there. Ben made you some breakfast. Isn't that nice?"

"Yes, that's nice. Thank you. Were y'all talking about me?"

"Why don't you come sit down?" Celeste said, patting the stool next to her.

Tabatha walked over and sat down as Ben slid a plate in front of her. She looked down at it as if she was assessing whether she wanted to take a bite, but she finally did.

"So what's going on?"

"I'm going to leave you two ladies to chat. I'll check in later," he said, slipping out of the room quickly.

Celeste turned slightly on her stool, unsure of how to start this conversation. What was she supposed to say to this young woman who wasn't even her daughter? What business was it of hers, really? But somebody had to do it. Somebody had to point out the elephant in the room, so to speak.

"I know I'm not your mother, and you might think I have no right to an opinion, but you have to make some decisions now, Tabatha. If you'd had your baby last night, what would you have done?"

She shrugged her shoulders. "I don't know."

"The reality is that you're either going to be a mother or you're not. If you choose to be a mother, we need to figure out your housing situation and get a nursery set up. If you're not, you need to have time to choose the right parents for your baby."

"How am I supposed to choose parents? I don't even have parents!" she said, throwing her hands up.

“I know this is hard…"

"Do you? Do you know what it's like to have your body violated, get pregnant and then be forced into making decisions you're not ready to make? Don't you know that this entire nine months I felt like a clock was ticking in the background? "

Celeste hated to see her so upset, but she knew this conversation had to happen. Somebody had to take the reins and help her. Walking on eggshells around her wasn’t a reasonable plan anymore.

"You know what? I don't know what it's like. And I'm so sorry that you've been put in this position through no fault of your own. It's not fair. But that doesn't take away the fact that decisions have to be made, and I'm trying to be the adult who helps you make those decisions. It's not just about what's best for the baby. It also is about what's best for you."

"What's best for me doesn't matter," Tabatha said, pushing her plate away and putting her forehead on the countertop.

Celeste rubbed her back. "Of course it matters. You didn't ask for this, Tabatha."

She sat up, tears streaming down her face. "I love my baby even if I didn't ask for this."

"I know you do."

"How can I think about giving her up?"

"Her?"

"It's a girl. I asked my doctor at my last ultrasound."

"Oh." Most pregnant women had a gender reveal party these days, but Tabatha's situation was very different. There was nothing to celebrate here when it came to a choice between giving her baby away or becoming a teenage mother.

"How can I just give her away to strangers like she doesn't matter?"

"Tabatha, giving your baby to a loving family who can afford the time and money to raise her isn't about not loving her. That's the ultimate kind of love."

"Do you really think that?"

"I do. Listen, I had parents who didn't care about raising me and just let me fall into a broken system of foster care. I wish I'd been placed for adoption so I could've had a family who really wanted me. My life would've been very different."

"I just don't want to make the wrong decision. I want to do what's best for her, but it hurts so bad to think about."

"Why don't we play out some scenarios?"

"Okay…"

"Let's say you do keep her. What happens the next day when you come home from the hospital? What do you do?"

"They make you come home the next day?"

"Most of the time, yes."

"That's crazy."

"Agreed. Now, where do you go?"

"Here?"

Celeste smiled slightly. "Tabatha, we let you stay here, but we all agreed this isn't a long-term fix, right? We can't have a baby here for good. We'd need to work with social services to find an apartment or some kind of living situation that would be long-term for both of you."

"Right."

"Would you work or go to school?"

"I'd like to go to school."

"And how would you pay for rent? Utilities? Food?"

"I don't know!" she said, getting more and more agitated. "I guess I wouldn't go to school, so I would just work."

"Without an education, your job possibilities will be limited. I think minimum wage is about seven-dollars and twenty-five cents an hour here. For a forty-hour work week, that's..."

"Two-hundred ninety dollars."

"You're smart. So, if we take out for taxes and such, let's say you make one-thousand dollars a month. Average rent for a one-bedroom in a decent area around here is about eleven-hundred dollars a month."

Tabatha's eyes widened. "Really?"

"Really."

Her shoulders fell a bit as the reality of the situation landed on her. Celeste hated to be so frank with her, but she knew a sixteen-year-old girl couldn't possibly understand what life would be like with a baby.

"I didn't know it was so expensive."

"I'm really not trying to convince you of anything. Honestly. I just want you to know the truth about what your life will look like if you keep the baby. You'll be a teenage single mother with no education and a minimum wage job. You can probably get government assistance of some kind, but that will be your life, at least for a while. Some people get out from under that with hard work, but who will watch the baby? Daycare? How would you pay for that?"

"I don't know," she said, staring off into space. "I don't want her to be raised like that. I want her to have the best life, ya know? I want her to go to ballet classes and school field trips. I want her to have a puppy and huge Christmas celebrations surrounded by family. I can't give her any of that."

Tears started to fall, and then Tabatha descended into sobs, her whole body rocked by the reality of it all.

"I'm so sorry, Tabatha," Celeste said, her arm around Tabatha's shoulder.

"I've been procrastinating this whole time about making a decision because I wanted to make it work.

Who wants to give up their child? I thought if I waited long enough, it would be easier, but it's not. I have to give her up because it's the only way she can have the best life. I can't give her that right now."

"Do you want me to call the social worker?"

Tabatha nodded through sobs. "Yes, please."

"I love this one!" Janine said, running her hand across the glossy white wood. She and William had been out looking at nursery furniture all morning before his first tour of the day.

"It's nice. What about the matching dresser and changing table?"

Janine was surprised at how excited he was. They didn't have unlimited money by any means, but William wasn't afraid to choose the best for their new baby.

"I like the whole set. Do you think we can get it?"

He smiled. "Yes. Let's do it. Plus, my mom gave us a gift." He opened his wallet and pulled out five crisp one-hundred-dollar bills.

"What? Dixie gave that to us?"

"Yes. She'd been saving it for the day we had our own child. Can you believe that?"

"I'm going to give her such a big hug when I see her! I have the best mother-in-law."

"Are you ready to purchase this set?" the saleswoman asked.

"Yes. Can we get it delivered today, by chance?" William asked. "We're adopting a baby, and it could be any day now."

The woman smiled broadly. "How exciting! Of course. I'll get our delivery guy scheduled for late this afternoon, if that works?"

Janine was so excited to get the nursery set up. She'd been waiting to do this for her whole life, and she was going to savor every moment from start to finish.

Julie and Dawson sat in the waiting area outside the counseling office, each of them reacting in different ways. While Julie's foot was tapping so fast it could've worn a hole through the carpet, Dawson was calm, cool and collected, as usual.

"The bell just rang, so as soon as the kids get to class, I'll call down to their teacher on the intercom," Mr. Rollins said, poking his head through the doorway.

Jacie's parents - whose names were Tom and Dana, Julie had learned - were sitting on the other side of the room. Nobody was making eye contact, and no words had even been exchanged between Tom and Dana. What a sad marriage they seemed to have.

A few minutes later, Dylan opened the door to the counseling office. A look of surprise fell over his face when he saw his parents.

"Mom? Dad? What're you doing here?"

"Hey, buddy. We've been talking to Mr. Rollins about a few things, and he thought you should be here."

Jacie opened the door shortly afterward, and that's when Dylan realized what was going on. He looked at his parents, so much upset on his face.

"What did you do?" he whispered.

"Is everyone ready?" Mr. Rollins asked, opening his door again.

The parents stood up and followed him back into the conference room with the children trailing behind, obviously not wanting to be there. Dylan sat beside Dawson and next to Mr. Rollins while Jacie's family sat on the other side of the table.

"Kids, we're here today because of an accusation of bullying. Do you both know that we do not allow bullying at our school?" He looked at each of them, and they both nodded. "Does anybody have something they want to say?"

Julie raised her hand. "I do."

"I meant the children, Mrs. Lancaster."

She shrugged her shoulders. "Right."

Dylan slowly raised his hand.

"Okay, Dylan. What would you like to say?"

He stood up. "I would like to say that Jacie Mays is the meanest girl I've ever met. She's meaner than that snake my daddy caught near the marsh last year."

Dawson stifled a laugh, but it sounded like he was about to pop. Julie elbowed him.

"Well, you're the dumbest boy I've ever met!" Jacie said, standing up and balling up her fists at her sides. Her mother pulled on her shirt and made her sit back down.

"You think this is funny?" Dana, Jacie's mother, said, her eyes glaring at Dawson.

"No, m'am. Of course not." He continued to pinch his lips together. Julie didn't think any of this was funny.

"Dylan, we don't say rude or mean things like that to each other," Mr. Rollins said. The man was very good at keeping his cool. "That, too, is bullying."

"She bullied me first by saying my birthmother didn't want me and that nobody really wanted me." His little voice quivered as he repeated her ugly words.

"That's 'cause he kept writing me poems and embarrassing me in front of my friends!" Jacie said, standing up again. She wiggled away as her mother tried to grab her shirt again.

"It was because I liked you, and I was trying to be all romantic, like in those silly movies my momma watches!"

"Well, I don't want no romance from a boy!"

"You could've just said so, but you had to be meaner than a rattlesnake!"

Everyone just looked back and forth at them, yelling like they were in a very rude tennis match, and poor Mr. Rollins quickly lost control.

"Kids! Stop it!"

His receptionist, Mona, poked her head through the doorway. "Everything okay in here?"

Quiet fell over the room. Mr. Rollins sucked in a sharp breath. "We're fine, Mona. No need for security... yet."

"Can I say something?"

To everyone's surprise, Jacie's dad stood up. His voice was soft and unassuming, and he looked quite terrified. Julie couldn't blame him. If she lived in the same house as his wife and daughter, she would live in fear every day.

"Of course, Mr. Mays," Mr. Rollins said, probably glad to get a break.

"My daughter can be a bit much. She gets that from her mother."

"Tom!"

He didn't make eye contact with his wife. "I want to say sorry to Dylan for the way she made fun of you. I know your birthmother loved you, and your parents adore you. That much is obvious."

"Thank you," Julie mouthed.

"I also know boys of Dylan's age don't understand social cues all that well. I did something similar at his age. I pursued a little girl who wanted no part of me. She, too, was mean as a rattlesnake. Luckily, one day she started liking those poems, but we were in high school by then." He looked over at his wife, who wasn't looking at him and had her arms crossed. He was obviously referring to when they met.

"Thank you, Mr. Mays," Mr. Rollins said. "I appreciate your input. Still, Dylan, I think we need to talk about boundaries a bit, okay?"

"Okay."

"When a young lady says she's not interested, you need to respect that. Do you understand?"

"Yes, but I was just trying to do what they do in the movies. Sometimes the girls play hard to get. I think that's what they called it."

Julie smiled. "Son, the movies aren't reality. Not all girls are the same, just like all boys aren't the same. When another person tells you to stop, you stop. That's called respecting someone's boundaries. Okay?"

"Yes, m'am."

"Now, Jacie, don't you have something to say?" Mr. Rollins asked.

She crossed her arms and furrowed her eyebrows. "Nope."

"Well, then, that's a problem because it shows an unwillingness to change your bullying behavior. Are you sure you don't want to say you're sorry about what you said?"

"Nope," she said again.

Her mother poked her. "Jacie! Say something."

Jacie shook her head.

"Mr. Rollins, I think our daughter needs some time away from her friends," Mr. Mays said.

"Tom!"

"For a long time, I've thought it would be good

for Dana and Jacie to spend more time together. Dana recently lost her job, so this is as good a time as any for a little homeschooling."

"Tom…" Dana warned.

"Maybe the rest of the school year."

"Tom!" Suddenly, Mrs. Mays didn't seem to have any other words.

"Honey, our daughter needs this time with you because she's acting out in school to get attention," he said quietly. "You know that's what this is about."

"So, it's settled then. We won't have to suspend Jacie because she will be homeschooled for the remainder of the year. And Dylan understands more about boundaries in these kinds of situations, yes?"

"Yes, sir," Dylan said. He looked over at Julie with a slight smile on his face. It was obvious he was relieved that Jacie Mays wouldn't be back at school this year. "I'm sorry, Jacie. I didn't mean to do anything wrong." She turned her head and ignored him.

As they all left the office, Julie and Dawson hugged their son goodbye and watched him walk down the hall. Jacie and her mother quickly escaped to the parking lot while Mr. Mays waited behind for a moment.

"I really am sorry about what my daughter said to your son," he said, shaking Dawson's hand.

"Thank you."

"My wife is a bit... prickly. She hasn't always been this way, but when she lost her job, her personality changed. Jacie has picked up on that. She craves time with her mother, and Dana has been checked out a bit. I'm sorry this happened, but I hope Dylan has a better rest of his school year."

"We appreciate you speaking up and taking the lead on this," Julie said, shaking his hand too. What she really wanted to say was they appreciated him finally speaking at all.

CHAPTER 8

TABATHA WALKED SLOWLY DOWN THE SIDEWALK. After her night in the hospital, she probably should've stayed in bed for the day and rested, but her sixteen-year-old body wanted to move. To do something. It seemed the larger she got, the less she moved, but her brain was always fidgety. Restless.

She saw Janine was in the studio, and a class had just let out, so she decided to go inside. At first, Janine didn't see her come in. She was on the phone in her office, and Tabatha didn't want to interrupt, so she sat in one of the chairs in the small waiting area up front.

"It's so good to hear from you, Colleen. Did your mom tell you the good news? No? We're getting a baby!"

Tabatha smiled when she heard the excitement in Janine's voice. If anyone deserved this, it was her. She was a wonderful person and was going to make a great mother.

"Yes, and it's going to be later this week. Can you believe that? We're scrambling to get the nursery set up... No, we don't know the sex yet, but we don't care. We're going to be parents!"

After a few moments, Janine said her goodbyes and walked toward the front, startled to see Tabatha sitting there.

"Oh, wow, you scared me!" she said, holding her hand to her chest.

"Sorry. I came in as the last class was letting out, and then you were on the phone so..."

"You heard my news?" Janine asked, a broad smile on her face.

"I did."

"I'm just bursting with excitement. I can hardly teach classes because I just want to go to every baby store and buy cute stuff." Realizing who she was talking to, Janine seemed to pull back a bit on her energy. "How are you doing?"

"I went into false labor last night, so I spent the night in the hospital."

Janine reached down and touched her shoulder.

"Oh, sweetie, I know that had to be tough. What did the doctor say?"

"That I'm still due in four to five weeks, and I should take it easy."

"Bed rest?"

"Not really. Just be chill, I guess."

Janine smiled. "How about I teach you some breathing exercises to help with Braxton Hicks contractions?"

"There are breathing exercises? That would've been good to know last night," she said, laughing.

Tabatha followed Janine into the practice room. Janine handed her a rolled up yoga mat, but Tabatha just laughed."

"You don't really think I can bend over and roll this out, do you?"

Janine put her hand over her eyes. "Sorry about that. My brain isn't operating on all cylinders today."

She took the yoga mat back from Tabatha and rolled it out on the floor. Tabatha eased herself down, being careful not to completely topple over backwards.

"I think it's cute how excited you are about the baby."

"I feel bad even talking about it in front of you, honestly. I know you're struggling."

Tabatha shrugged her shoulders. "I have to make some decisions, and quickly. Going to the hospital last night just drove that point home. I can't keep dragging my feet about this."

"Do you know which way you're leaning?"

"I think adoption. I don't see any way for me to raise a baby on my own at sixteen. It wouldn't be good for her or for me."

"I know this has to be hard, Tabatha. I hope nobody's putting pressure on you."

"They aren't. Everybody's just trying to get me to decide because time is running out. I understand their point. I thought by now the decision would be easy to make, but it's harder because I do love my baby."

"I know you do," Janine said, reaching over and taking her hand. "Your baby can feel that. She knows you love her, and you will love her for the rest of your life. Hopefully, you can find a family that will allow you to be involved, if you want."

"Is that what you're going to do with your birth mother?"

"I think so. We haven't gotten a lot of details about her and what she wants. We're sort of in a waiting game right now. In fact, I had expected to hear from my social worker by now, but I'm sure she's busy."

"I'm thrilled for you, Janine. You're going to be a great mother. That baby is lucky."

Janine smiled. "Thank you. Now, let's get on with those breathing exercises, so you aren't in so much pain if this happens again."

Abigail stood on Griffin's front porch, this time without a sick puppy. Instead, she was carrying two reusable tote bags full of groceries. Anytime she could try to help the environment by not using plastic, she did.

Griffin had asked her to purchase the ingredients, although she wasn't exactly sure what he was making. Abigail wasn't picky when it came to food, thankfully.

She knocked on the door and waited. She could hear Bingo barking inside, and when Griffin opened the door, Bingo lunged, putting his paws on her waist.

"I'm so sorry! I've been working with him on that, but I guess he got a little too excited when he saw you. He probably remembers you from the shelter."

"No problem. I obviously need to strengthen my ab muscles, though," she said, laughing.

Griffin wrangled Bingo into the house, ordering him to his kennel. He locked him inside temporarily so he could help Abigail get the groceries in.

"Were you able to get everything?"

"Yes, I was. Can I ask what we're having?"

Griffin took the grocery bags from her and set them on the counter. "I'm making my famous chicken fajitas with homemade corn tortillas and for dessert we're having flan."

"So it's Mexican night?"

"Yes, but my fajitas are much better than any restaurant you'll go to."

"So you're saying that if I go to an actual Mexican restaurant where people from Mexico prepare the food, your fajitas are still better? The guy from Nashville?" She started laughing.

Griffin put his hands on his hips. "Why do I feel like you're mocking me?"

"Because I am."

"Well, I'll just let you try my fajitas, and then you can eat your words. Of course, you'll be full from eating fajitas, so you might need to eat your words tomorrow."

She loved their banter. When they first met, she

hadn't liked him one bit. Of course, he had accused her of puppy kidnapping, so that wasn't exactly the best start to their friendship. But now, she really felt like they were at ease with each other. After spending the night together watching over the puppy, they had had a lot of time to talk about life and other things.

"How can I help?"

"How do you feel about cutting up onions and peppers?"

"I feel good about it. I really do."

Griffin laughed. "You're quite the sarcastic one."

"You know, I never was until I started spending more time with Celeste. I think she's rubbing off on me. I'm not sure that's a good thing."

He handed her an onion and a knife. "I can't wait to meet this Celeste. She sounds scary and interesting at the same time."

"I think that's a good way to describe her. Thankfully, she's easing up a bit now that she's been dating Ben."

"He's the pediatrician, right?"

"Right. He's a good guy. At first I didn't know what he saw in her, but they mesh well together. He calms her down a bit."

"It's always good to have balance in a relationship, I suppose."

"Very true."

"So, Abigail, do you have any hobbies?"

"I'm not really a hobby person. I enjoy helping the foster kids, of course. I like playing with my new puppy when she isn't eating chocolate."

He smiled. "Surely you have other activities you enjoy?"

She thought for a moment. "When I was young, I used to love to draw. I haven't done that in many years. And there was a while where I took horseback riding lessons. Not a lot of that going on around here."

"You know, I'm getting a couple of horses. A friend of mine runs a rescue out in Texas, so I agreed to take on a couple since I have this land."

"Really? That's amazing."

"I was thinking about using them for lessons, but also for people who need horse therapy."

"Oh, that's a wonderful idea."

Griffin put the strips of chicken into the frying pan before handing Abigail red and green peppers to cut up.

"Horse therapy has always been something that interested me. I had a friend who did that back in

Nashville, and I got to see firsthand just how important it was for people."

"I think that's great that you're thinking of bringing something like that to Seagrove."

"Maybe you can help train the horses."

"I don't have any experience training horses," she said, laughing. "I've only ridden a horse a few times."

"Well, maybe I can teach you how to ride horses, and you can learn how to train them. I mean, if you're interested in something like that."

"I'll give it some thought."

"So, are you planning on getting a job outside of what you're doing with the foster kids?"

She used her knife to slide the peppers across the cutting board to get them out of her way. "Yeah, I really need to. We only do the stuff for foster kids at limited times throughout the year, and I certainly don't make any money from it. Even though Elaine left us quite a bit of money to get started, it's not enough to live on for the rest of our lives. Celeste and I are both going to have to get jobs."

"What kind of work are you looking for?"

"Honestly, I'd love something with animals. I thought about applying at the shelter, but I know they don't usually need that many employees to keep it running."

"I'd like to throw something out at you," he said, stopping what he was doing and leaning against the counter.

"Okay…"

"Well, as you could see when you came over with Petunia, I am sorely in need of somebody to run my front desk. I was going to write up a job listing next week, but if you'd be interested…"

She held up her hand. "You don't have to do that. I have literally no experience, and you should probably find somebody who knows what they're doing."

"Didn't you tell me you used to work in a big public relations firm?"

"Well, yes. But I don't have any experience being a front desk person or working with animals."

He chuckled. "Trust me, I think you have more than enough experience to do the job here. But I totally understand if you don't want to work with me every day. I mean, I can be a pain in the rear end occasionally."

"You're actually offering me a job?"

"I am actually offering you a job, yes."

Abigail considered it for a long moment. What would it be like to work with him every day? They were obviously getting along, and she still wasn't completely sure if this was a date. What if they did start dating? Then she would be dating her boss. What kind of idea was that?

Still, she needed a job, and he was offering one. She would love to work with animals every single day. What better job could there be, short of being a veterinarian herself?

"You know what? I think I'll take you up on that."

"You don't even know what I'm offering for pay," Griffin said, laughing.

“Oh. Yeah, I suppose I should’ve asked that.”

“Don’t worry, it’ll be good. We can work out the details after dinner. Sound good?”

“Sure. You know, I never thought about one coincidence.”

“What?”

“The public relations firm where I worked… it was also in Nashville. That means we were there at the same time.”

“Really? Where was your office?”

“Do you know where that big bookstore is with the cafe outside? And the building with the revolving door is right next to it?”

“I know exactly where that is. I used to have coffee at the bookstore every morning before I opened my office because it was just a block over.”

Her eyes widened. "I had coffee there every morning, too."

Griffin smiled. "Wow. Who would've thought we didn't meet all those mornings in Nashville, but we ended up meeting in an animal shelter all the way in Seagrove, South Carolina?"

"So funny."

"Maybe it was fate," he said, offhandedly. But she couldn't help but think that maybe it actually was.

Tabatha sat across from the social worker at the giant wooden table. She felt like she was in a royal family having dinner.

"Have you considered the option of keeping your baby?" the woman, named DeeDee, asked.

"Yes, I've considered it, but at my age, I don't think it'd be good for me or my baby."

"How certain are you that adoption is the right fit?"

Tabatha looked over at Celeste, who had come with her for moral support. "Just be honest, honey."

Tabatha looked down at her ever-expanding belly. "Maybe ninety-five percent. There will always be a part of me that was never sure."

"Understandable. A lot of birth mothers say something similar."

"I just want her to have the best life possible, and I can't provide that. I need to get my life straight, and I'm not dragging my kid through that."

"I think you're making a very brave decision, Tabatha. Now, you have a couple of options. There's a completely private adoption where once you sign over rights, you don't see the baby again. There are no letters or pictures. It's a very clean break. There is also open adoption, and you will decide with the adoptive parents how open it is. There will usually be pictures and letters, and some will allow visits. Have you given thought to what you'd want?"

"Open. I definitely want to know how my baby is doing."

"Good. Okay, I do have some files to show you then. We have many potential adoptive parents waiting. This first file is a couple that lives about an hour from here. The mother would stay at home with the baby and her other children..."

"I don't want someone with other children. I want the focus to be on my baby."

"Oh. Okay. Well, that certainly narrows the field a bit..." She looked through her files and slid most of them to the side. "Here's one that you may like. They live a couple of hours from here, and the husband is a police officer. The mother..."

"I don't want either of the parents to have a dangerous job. I lost my father young, and I don't want my baby to have to go through that."

"Tabatha, you may not find the perfect family..." Celeste offered.

"I have to. This is my child. I can't send her somewhere that isn't safe for her."

"Why don't I take a day or so to talk to some of my colleagues outside of this area and see if we can't find the right fit? Can I call you tomorrow?"

Tabatha nodded and stood up, her stomach protruding over the table. Time was running out, that was for sure.

"Thank you for taking the time with us today," Celeste said.

"It's my job, and I love it," Dee Dee said, smiling.

"You love watching mothers have to give their babies away?" Tabatha asked, glaring at her.

"Tabatha..." Celeste started to say.

"It's okay. Look, I know how hard this is. I've worked with many birth mothers in my career. I should've worded that better. I love helping my mamas find the best families for their babies. I don't love the situation that brings them here. I'm sorry for how I said that."

"Thank you," Tabatha said, feeling raw inside and out. She just couldn't get her emotions under control. It felt like everybody around her was fine, just living their lives like nothing was happening. Meanwhile, every day she held her baby inside was part of a long goodbye. As much as she was sick of being fat and swollen, if she could hold her baby inside forever, she would. As it was, she was saying goodbye every single moment of every single day. It was horrible. How could the world keep spinning while she was waiting for the moment her baby would be taken away from her?

CHAPTER 9

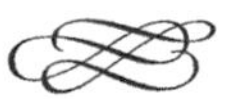

"A PROM?" DAWSON ASKED, TAKING A SIP OF HIS coffee.

"Yep," Ben replied, a proud smile on his face.

"You really are trying to woo this woman, aren't you?"

"Yep."

"My wife is going to love this. I bet she makes me wear a tuxedo."

Ben laughed. "So, we can have it here?"

"It's pretty short notice, but if you think you can get it together that fast, sure. Have it here. We'll do it out on this deck. It's beautiful at night with the lights and the moon over the ocean."

"Thanks, man. I owe you one."

"You owe me way more than one."

Ben took a bite of his croissant. "How do you figure?"

"Remember that time in school when I agreed to give Heather Hilton that poem you wrote for her, only the teacher confiscated it before I could? She then read it in front of the whole class, and everybody laughed. I was humiliated. By the way, you're a horrible poet. I hope you've stopped doing that."

"Roses are red, violets are blue..."

"Please stop."

"Well, hello there. Am I interrupting the boys club meeting?" Julie asked, walking outside with a plate of fruit.

"Yes, you are. We're planning a prom. Doesn't that sound masculine?" Dawson joked.

"A prom?"

"It seems that Ben is wooing Celeste quite seriously, and she never got to go to her prom. So, we're hosting a prom right here on this deck in an effort to improve Ben's love life and hopefully get him married off one day."

Ben slapped him on the arm. "You're making me sound like a wuss."

"Then my work here is done," Dawson said, standing up. "I have to get over to the lumberyard. I'm making a dinner table for the Elbert family, and I need a few more pieces." He kissed Julie on the top of her head and walked toward his truck. "See you at the prom, Ben!"

"Sorry about him. He thinks he's funny, and I don't have the heart to tell him the truth," Julie said, sitting down. Ben laughed.

"That's the thing. Sometimes he *is* funny, but I don't want to tell him. That would just encourage him."

"So, you're planning a prom? What do you have in mind?"

Ben sat there for a long moment. "Um, well… I mean music. Maybe some chips…"

Julie put her hand on her forehead. "Chips, Ben? That's your big plan?"

"To be honest, I haven't gotten much further than the venue."

"When are you planning to do this?"

"Friday night?"

Julie's mouth fell open. "*This* Friday night?"

"Yeah."

"Oh, Ben. Why so soon?"

"Trying to align my schedule with Celeste's and your very popular inn's schedule… well, it was difficult."

She sucked in a deep breath and blew it out.

"Okay, I'm going to help you."

"Thank the good Lord."

"First off, I know a great DJ. I'll call him today. We need food, so what about a big country buffet? Lucy can handle all of that."

"I love Lucy," Ben said, quickly realizing what he'd just said.

Julie rolled her eyes. "Anyway, what about Celeste's dress?"

He froze for a moment. "I was thinking this could be a surprise?"

"How are you going to get her to dress up?"

"I have no idea."

"Hmm... Let me think a minute... I know! I'll invite her to a fake charity event for foster kids. I'll tell her it's very formal. Do you think that would work?"

"Maybe. She'd do anything for those kids."

"Okay, so it's settled. I'll make a fake invitation and deliver it to her today. Hopefully, she'll say yes. Oh, and I'll tell Abigail the truth so she can help me."

Ben smiled. "You really are a good plotter, Julie. Maybe I should warn Dawson."

Julie stood up, ready to walk toward the house. "Oh, honey, he knows. Trust me."

"A charity event? Why such late notice?" Celeste asked, staring down at the invitation Julie had just handed her at her front door.

"Yeah, sorry. I thought I'd sent them all out, but a few fell between the seats in my car on the way to the post office. So weird."

Celeste stared at it a moment longer and then shrugged her shoulders. "I guess I can come. It says formal, but I don't have anything formal."

"Davenport's has a lovely selection of dresses."

The last thing she wanted to do was go dress shopping since it was hard to find ones that fit her tall stature, but Celeste was willing to do whatever it took for the foster kids. As she said goodbye to Julie and closed the door, she saw her meet Abigail on the sidewalk and hand her an invitation, also.

"What was that about?" Tabatha asked from the living room. She was sitting on the sofa, a pile of file folders in front of her on the coffee table.

"Oh, just a party I need to attend on Friday. Having any luck?"

"These people all seem like duds. I mean, look at this guy. He's an accountant. I don't want my kid raised by an accountant."

Celeste laughed. "And why is that?"

"Can you imagine how boring that is? He'd probably start quizzing my kid about tax rates and deductions before she could even walk."

"I doubt that."

"And look at this woman. She has a scowl on her face in every picture. Aren't they supposed to try to impress me with the pictures? She's scary. No, thank you." She tossed two more folders onto the floor beside her.

"You're starting to run out of couples there, aren't you?"

"I'm not just going to choose some random couple to take my baby. I need them to have certain qualities."

"Such as?"

She sat back against the sofa and crossed her arms over her expanding belly. "Well, they need to be active, energetic, outdoorsy, artsy…"

"Interesting combo, but that doesn't necessarily make them good parents."

"They should be kind, loving, responsible and mature."

"Better."

"These people don't look half bad, but they live in a condo." She handed the picture to Celeste.

"So? What's wrong with a condo?"

"There's probably no backyard, and a kid needs a yard. Plus, they have a cat."

"And?"

"I'm allergic to cats, and I bet my kid will be too."

"I'm not sure that's how it works."

"Ugh!" Tabatha tossed all the folders back onto the table and sighed, laying her head back against the sofa. "Why is this so hard?"

"Because you're making the biggest decision of your life, and you're scared to make the wrong one. Just know that the social workers have vetted these people. They've visited their homes, run background checks, and made sure they're all good potential parents. No couple is going to be perfect for your child, Tabatha. That's because you love her, and nobody will ever be good enough for her."

She smiled slightly. "You may be right about that."

Celeste picked up the stack again and set it on Tabatha's lap. "I think it's worth taking a second look at some of these."

She sat up and started thumbing through the files again. "I guess this couple isn't so bad. He's a history teacher, and she plans to be a stay-at-home mom. They like to travel, and she teaches piano lessons on the side at her house."

"They sound wonderful."

"Yeah. I guess it wouldn't hurt to meet them."

"That's a great idea, Tabatha."

As Celeste said it, she felt an unfamiliar pain in her heart. Tabatha had become like a daughter to her, and watching her give up a baby was heart wrenching. Still, she knew she was making the right decision, but that didn't make her hurt any less for Tabatha. This was going to be a long road of grief, no matter what couple she chose.

Janine stood in the center of the small room and turned all the way around, taking in each and every part of it. She was going to be a mommy in a few days. The birthmother was almost at her due date, and she was anxious to meet her, but not until the nursery was complete. It just needed a few finishing touches.

"I think it looks great!" Julie said, putting her arm around Janine.

"It really is lovely," SuAnn said. "You are going to put a little more color on that bookshelf, aren't you?"

Janine rolled her eyes. "Mother, just let me have a nice moment, okay?"

"It's just darling, Janine. And it will work for a boy or a girl," Dixie said, smiling. Janine loved this moment. She was sharing the biggest time in her life with her sister, mother, and mother-in-law. It was just so special to her.

"So, have you met the birthmother yet?" SuAnn asked, straightening a picture on the wall that didn't need to be straightened.

"No. She keeps changing the plan. It's a little unnerving, but I'm sure she's under a lot of stress."

"I'm sure that's what it is," Julie said, reassuringly. "She chose you and William, so you know she's serious."

"Of course. I'm just having a lot of anxiety. This came on so quickly."

"It's going to be great, honey. You and William are going to be wonderful parents," Dixie said. She was always so uplifting, and Janine adored her. She couldn't wait to watch Dixie become a grandmother since she'd never been one before. Some kid was going to be very blessed.

And then there was SuAnn, who had been a grandmother twice before with Meg and Colleen. She'd done a good job, and Janine was excited to let her child grow up, running back and forth between the bookstore, the yoga studio and the bakery. What a great life.

When Janine really let herself think too hard, she wondered if she really would be a good mother. Her mother had been good, but her relationships with Julie and Janine had been rocky, to say the least. Then there was Janine's trauma, and although she had dealt with it, there were still parts of her soul that got re-traumatized on occasion.

Still, she had love to give. Massive amounts of it. She also had patience, kindness, and the best husband on the planet. She'd be able to teach her child about yoga, meditation, and emotions. He'd teach their child about the outdoors, conservation, and respecting all the creatures of the marsh and the ocean.

When Janine imagined their lives together as a family, she thought about picnics at the beach, rides in the boat on the marsh, and Sunday dinners with Dixie and the rest of the family.

"What do you think?" Julie asked.

"Huh?"

"Were you lost in thought again?"

Janine smiled. "Sorry. My brain feels like I have twenty tabs open, and it's about to shut down completely."

"Then it sounds like you need a fun night out, darlin'!" Dixie interjected.

"Huh?"

"We're apparently going to the prom," SuAnn said, rolling her eyes.

"Stop being a stick in the mud, Mom. It'll be fun," Julie said.

"What are y'all talking about?" Janine asked, still confused.

"I was trying to explain before you stared off into space and disappeared for a couple of minutes. Basically, we're throwing a prom at the inn for Celeste. Ben is surprising her since she never went to prom. She thinks it's a fancy benefit for foster kids, but we all know the truth. So, get a dress and be at the inn on Friday night at seven."

"What if I have a baby by then?"

"I guess you gotta get a tiny tux or itty bitty sequin gown!" Dixie said, laughing as she slapped her on the back.

Abigail stood at the counter, looking down at the very large Great Dane that was standing in front of her, almost at eye level.

"So, what are we seeing Duke for today?"

"He ate a sock. And possibly half of a ball of yarn," the woman said, hanging her head.

"Wow. Sounds like Duke isn't getting enough food," she said, trying to make a joke. The woman didn't crack a smile.

"Are you saying I don't feed my dog properly?"

Abigail cleared her throat. "No, ma'am. That was my lame attempt at making a joke. Sorry about that. Have a seat, and I'll let Dr. Connor know you're here."

She walked out from behind the counter and into Griffin's tiny office. He was finishing up notes on the computer from the previous patient.

"Oh, hey. Is my next patient here?"

"Yes. Duke the Great Dane ate a sock and some yarn. Oh, and his owner doesn't have a very good sense of humor."

He smiled. "What did you say?"

She scrunched her nose. "I might have said maybe he wasn't getting enough food. It was a joke."

Griffin stood up, holding an iPad in his hand. "A little piece of advice. When someone is worried about their animal, keep the jokes to a minimum. People are on edge when they come to the vet."

"I wasn't trying to..."

"I know, but think about when you brought Petunia here with chocolate poisoning. If I'd made a joke, would you have laughed?"

She thought for a moment. "No. I would've slugged you."

Griffin laughed as he walked past her toward the door. "I'd like to believe that's not true."

Her first day at work was proving to be more stressful than she thought. First, she had to help Griffin hold down a very upset cat who needed her eyes examined. Then she helped him cut the nails of a pit bull who wanted no part of it. She's experienced smells she had never smelled before. There were weird liquids on the floor that needed to be cleaned up throughout the day. It was all very different from her previous cushy office job, but so far, she loved it.

Something about being around animals all day was filling her well in a way working in PR never did. She felt like she was doing something that mattered, and it didn't hurt that she got to work with Griffin all day.

She wasn't sure what their relationship was just yet. Maybe it was just friendship, or maybe it was growing into something more. Sometimes she thought she knew, and other times she didn't have a clue. He hadn't made a move on her at all. No hand holding. No kissing. Not even a quick hug.

But it still felt like something was there. She didn't know what to call it, and now he was her boss. Maybe nothing would ever come of it, and she'd become "Old Lady Clayton", the one who lives in the big house that the kids are scared to pass.

Abigail had always loved animals. Even when she was a little girl, she had always wanted a puppy or a kitten. She even went through a time where she wanted one of those tiny little monkeys that would sit on her shoulder. Her dad had told her no, and that was that.

Then she went into foster care, and the families she stayed with either didn't have dogs at all, or they had something like a fish. Who thought that a fish was a pet?

Working at a veterinary clinic was an interesting job so far. Sure, there were smells and liquids, but there were also the most adorable animals coming in and out of the door all day. It was very hard to be in a bad mood when you were getting to hug squishy little puppies.

Working in public relations had been a whole different ballgame. Most of the time, she was sitting at a desk wearing a stuffy business suit, taking phone calls from people she didn't want to talk to. It wasn't exactly the most exciting job, but she had been thankful to have it.

Seagrove was a different kind of town. Although she was sure there were public relations businesses somewhere around, probably closer to Charleston, she had no desire to work for them. Elaine had given her a new start at life. She had given her the ability to choose what she wanted to do with her life without giving thought to the practicality of it.

"He's going to be just fine, " she heard Griffin say, as he walked Duke and his owner to the door.

"Thank you, Dr. Connor. We saw your grandfather for years, and I'm glad he passed the business onto you. We'll see you in a few months for Duke's next set of shots."

The woman walked out the door and got into her car, wrangling her giant dog, that looked more like a horse. Abigail had never seen a dog so big. She was pretty sure the canine needed a saddle.

"He's a big boy, huh?" she said, leaning against the counter. Griffin laughed.

"I think he's the biggest patient we have, unless a cougar or gorilla comes in." He walked over to the counter and picked up the sign-in clipboard. "So, when's my next patient?"

"You actually have a thirty-minute break."

"Really? Wow! What ever will I do with so much free time?"

"Take up knitting? Write your first novel?"

Griffin smiled. "What makes you think it'd be my first novel?"

"Oh, yeah? A man of many talents?"

He chuckled. "You never know. Although I did almost fail English in high school, but that was because Maryanne Gladney sat beside me, and she was not a woman to be ignored."

Abigail crossed the previous patient's name off the clipboard sheet. "Is that who you took to prom?"

"Lord no. She had no time for me. She was the cheerleading captain and very popular, if you know what I mean. I was short, chubby and my dermatologist's best customer."

"Oh, please." She had a hard time believing he was ever anything but handsome.

"I'm serious. I was considered a bit of a nerd back in those days. I did end up going to my senior prom, but it was with a girl I thought I was doing a favor."

"What do you mean?"

"Aggie Harper was her name. She was even nerdier than I was. Captain of the math squad..."

"Yikes."

"Science club treasurer..."

"This is only getting worse."

"I felt bad for her, so when she asked me to prom, I said yes. I found out later she asked me on a dare and was basically forced to go with me."

Abigail poked out her bottom lip and reached across the counter to squeeze his shoulder. "Aw, you poor thing. Well, you eventually shed your nerd persona. I would've never known."

"That's because you haven't spent much time with me. Trust me, once I get to know you better, I'll start spewing useless trivia and facts that will reveal my nerdy alter ego."

Abigail laughed. "Can't wait."

"So, did you go to prom?"

"No. I wasn't very popular in school either. Nobody paid me much attention."

He looked at her. "Well, I bet you get a lot of attention now."

Abigail's face started to turn red. "Not really, but thanks."

"Did you hear about the prom at the inn?"

"I did. Celeste is going to be ecstatic and shocked."

"Are you going?"

"I kind of have to. I mean, she's my roommate, and everybody I know is going. Were you invited?"

"Actually, I was. I met Dawson at the hardware store and Julie at the bookstore, and both of them invited me."

She smiled. "That's how Seagrove works. Everybody knows everybody, and nobody is ever left out. It's like an anomaly on this planet."

"I was just wondering something."

"What?"

Now he was turning red. "Do you have a date to prom, Abigail Clayton?"

"I do not."

"Would you like to go with me, by chance?"

Why were her insides twisting in a knot? This was probably just a nice guy trying to do a kind thing. Not necessarily a date.

"I'd like that," she said, trying not to break out into a full-blown grin.

"Really? You'd go with me?"

"Why do you seem so surprised?"

"I don't know. I guess there's still a whole lot of that nerdy kid in here," he said, pointing to his heart.

"I'd be honored to go. I need to find a dress, though. Ben certainly didn't give all of us very much time to make a plan."

"Well, you can't blame the guy. He's trying to woo Celeste. It's actually a pretty slick move, if you ask me."

Before they could continue their conversation, the next patient arrived early. A tiny poodle with eye problems.

"I better go hide in my office so you can check them in," he whispered before slipping away down the side hallway.

CHAPTER 10

"It's official. I look like a circus tent." Tabatha stood in front of the full-length mirror in the dress store, her shoulders slouched forward.

"You certainly do not. I think that one looks great on you!" Janine said. She had offered to take Tabatha dress shopping since she needed to get one herself and Celeste was busy.

"I don't know why I agreed to go to this thing. I've never even been to a school dance, and I don't have a date. There aren't many guys who would want to take out a life-sized elephant."

Janine pinched her arm. "Stop saying things like that! You look beautiful. Pregnant women are gorgeous. You have a glow about you."

"It's not a glow. It's sweat. This dress is thicker than a sweater."

The sales lady smiled at Janine. "Why don't we go into the dressing room and take that one off? I might have something you likc a little better."

"Can I just go naked? It's so hot."

Janine laughed as she watched Tabatha walk to the back. She was getting rather large, especially for her height. But Janine would've done anything to have felt pregnancy. She was too old for that now, at least in her opinion, and adoption was her best route to becoming a mother.

Any day now, she would get a call from the social worker to come to the hospital and get her new baby. She couldn't wait. She still didn't know the gender, and that made it even more exciting.

It was concerning that the birth mother had chosen not to meet with them until they came to the hospital. She really expected they would have some time together, getting to know one another, before the birth. But everybody was different, and pregnant women tended to be more on the emotional side, anyway.

She would not do anything to push the birth mother into doing something she didn't want to do. Janine couldn't imagine how hard it was to give up a baby, which was one reason why she felt so much empathy for Tabatha.

What was it like to be sixteen years old, have no parents, and to be pregnant through no fault of your own? What kind of strength did it take for her to make the decision to give her baby up for adoption? Even though she was young, it didn't mean that she didn't love her child and want to keep her.

"This one doesn't suck as bad," Tabatha said, walking out of the dressing room. She sounded like every teenage girl Janine had ever met.

"Well, that's a ringing endorsement."

"I think it'll work. I'm not exactly going to be dancing the night away."

"You look beautiful," Janine said, smiling as she stood behind her while they looked in the mirror. For a moment, she thought about whether her baby might be a girl. Would she one day stand behind her own daughter, picking out wedding dresses?

Okay, maybe she was getting a little ahead of herself.

"Well, I've already picked out my dress, so why don't you go change back into your regular clothes and we can get out of here?"

"Okay," Tabatha said, obviously exhausted. She only had a few weeks left herself, and her OB/GYN wasn't even sure if she would make it that far. Being so small in stature, there was a good chance she would go into labor earlier than that.

They rang up their purchases, Janine offering to pay for Tabatha's dress, and walked out onto the sidewalk. The sun was piercing today. It was starting to get hot in Seagrove, and when summer came, it would be pretty miserable.

Not only would it be hot and humid, but that's when all the bugs came out. Janine hated getting bit all the time, and William was attacked every day on his job of doing tours in the marsh.

Still, neither of them would ever want to live anywhere else. Seagrove was home, and she couldn't wait to build a family there. Watching her child go off for his or her first day of preschool. Having picnics in the square, sitting on the green grass. Riding in the boat and showing their child everything that the low country had to offer.

There would be county fairs and school plays. Beach days and exploring the lighthouse. There was so much to look forward to that Janine had a hard time keeping up with all of it in her head. Secretly, she had started keeping a list of things she wanted to experience with her new child. It was kind of like a parent bucket list.

"I'm getting my hair and makeup done over at the salon before the prom. Would you like to join me?"

Tabatha shook her head. "That's okay. I'm really not trying to impress anybody. It's not like I have a date or will be dating anybody anytime soon." She sat down on one of the park benches surrounding the square.

"What's wrong?"

"I'm a teenager, and I'm probably never going to date again."

Janine smiled. "What are you talking about?"

"I'm doomed. If I had kept the baby, no guy was going to want to be with me. But even when I give the baby up for adoption, what guy is going to want to be with me then? The girl who gave her baby away? That's what my new label will be. Everybody already knows that I'm pregnant, and I'm going to go back to school without a baby. I might as well just move out of town and try to start over again."

Janine put her arm around Tabatha's shoulders. "You're overthinking this. People are going to think that you are very courageous for giving your child the life you can't give her right now. That is the essence of love, Tabatha. I hope you can see that one day."

Tabatha laid her head on Janine's shoulder and

quietly cried for a few moments before drying her tears and acting like nothing happened. She was a tough girl. She had to be.

As they drove over the bridge onto Seagrove Island, Celeste second-guessed her decision to go to this charity event. She wasn't much of a dancer, and she always thought she looked like an overdressed tree when she put on formalwear.

Sometimes, she loved being tall. Other times, like now, she wished that she could put on a pair of high heels and not touch the clouds. Instead, she had opted for flats with little rhinestones on them for effect.

"Are you excited?"

She looked over at Ben, who was wearing a tuxedo and looked awfully handsome.

"Not really. These kinds of events are typically stuffy. I mean, I'm glad it's being held at the inn, so at least I can sneak inside and hide if I need to. But I'll do anything to support the foster children. Plus, I'm pretty sure they want some of my money because they know about Elaine's inheritance."

"Or maybe they just like you and want you to be there."

She reached over and pinched his cheek. "Aren't you cute? People don't like me, Ben. They tolerate me. But they don't like me."

"I think that's a story you're telling yourself, Celeste. People do like you when you open up and show them who you really are. I swear, I'm going to knock down that strong outer wall of yours if it's the last thing I do."

He always told her she was too tough. She needed to let people in. But letting people in was the scariest thing she could imagine. Bungee jumping? Not a problem. Jumping out of an airplane? She would do it in a heartbeat. Public speaking while naked and holding a spider? Sign her up. But being vulnerable with people? No, thank you.

"Well, here we are," Ben said, pulling up a little further from the house than she thought would be typical.

"Why are we parking all the way over here?"

"Oh, I saw Dawson earlier. He asked that all the family members and close friends parked down here by the trees just so that some of the other guests could get the closer parking."

"I see. So family and friends don't count as much

as the big donors? Typical," she grumbled as she opened her door and stepped out. Ben ran around the car, as he usually did, trying to open her door before she could. This time, she was too fast for him.

"Can we try to have a nice evening? You might be surprised at how much you enjoy this."

"I doubt it. But again, you're cute for thinking so," she said, laughing.

Ben reached down and took her hand. They started walking toward the inn, and Celeste noticed that things looked different from what they normally did at these types of events. There were a lot more lights on the deck, and there appeared to be a DJ. This was different from any charity event she had been to before. Maybe things were unique in Seagrove.

She stopped in her tracks a moment later when she read the banner hanging over the dance floor area on the deck. It read "Celeste's First Prom" in big gold letters with a navy blue background. Tiny little twinkle lights framed the sign and most of the railings and inside of the tent area. Her breath caught in her throat.

"What... is... this?" she choked out after a long pause. She looked at Ben, who was beaming.

"Your first prom."

"I can't believe..."

He faced her and took both her hands. "Don't be mad. I know you don't like being the center of this kind of attention, but I was trying to think up the ultimate date, and this seemed pretty dang ultimate."

"You did all of this for me?"

"I had a lot of help."

"But this was your idea?"

"Yes. Are you mad?"

She felt tears starting to form. It felt foreign to her. "No, I'm not mad. Just shocked."

He ran his thumb across her cheek. "You shouldn't be shocked that I want to do nice things for you. That I want to make you smile. You deserve all the good things, Celeste. Just because your childhood sucked, and most people didn't care, doesn't mean your adulthood should suck too. I've made it my personal mission to make up for all the idiots in your life who didn't realize how amazing you are."

Now she wanted to burst into tears and dissolve into a puddle on the ground, but she couldn't. After all, her prom was waiting.

Julie swayed to the beat in Dawson's arms. She loved nights like this where they were outside under the moon, hearing the ocean waves in the background. And it helped that he was a pretty good dancer for a man as tall and muscular as he was.

"I think this came off without a hitch," she said, smiling up at him.

"I believe so. I'm not exactly an experienced party planner, but I think I helped Ben a little bit."

She laughed. "You helped him a lot. Y'all threw together an entire prom in less than a week. That's pretty impressive!"

"On another note, my feet are killing me in these shoes. These were not made for dancing."

She looked down at his tight fitting oxford dress shoes. "I don't think those fit you very well. Did you get the wrong size? The laces look like they're about to explode."

"This was the biggest size they had, and I was in kind of a pinch. I'm pretty sure I'm going to have blisters all over my feet."

"I love the slow songs because I get to dance with you," Julie said, squeezing him tighter.

"How much wine have you had, my dear wife?"

She giggled. "Enough."

"For what it's worth, I love dancing with you, too.

We don't do it nearly enough. I remember when we were first together, we would dance in the kitchen until the wee hours of the morning."

"Yeah, that was before Dylan. I swear if we make any kind of noise in the house at all, that kid comes running."

Dawson chuckled. "He's a good kid. I'm glad we got the whole bullying thing squared away."

"Yeah, but I do worry about the future. I don't want him to always be picked on because he was in foster care. I just don't understand kids who can say things like that."

"I don't either. Hey, is that Tabatha over there?"

Julie turned her head to the right and saw Tabatha standing on the corner of the deck, drinking a cup of punch.

"She looks so uncomfortable in that dress. I know I would've never wanted to wear sequins at almost nine months pregnant."

"I imagine if I was nine months pregnant, I would just want to walk around naked all the time. Who cares what people think?"

Julie laughed loudly, which got Tabatha's attention. She waved at her to come over, and she and Dawson stopped dancing. Dawson took the chance to sit down in a chair nearby and rest his feet.

"How are you enjoying prom?"

Tabatha shrugged her shoulders. "I tried to tell Celeste that I look like a circus tent, but now I think I just look like a very large disco ball."

Julie couldn't help but giggle at that. "I know how you feel. I gave birth to two daughters, one of which was the size of a watermelon. But you'll get past this, and you'll forget about all the terrible parts of pregnancy. You'll even forget the pain of labor."

"I think that matters more to women who keep their babies. Some biological thing that keeps you from hating your child for putting you through so much pain. Only problem is, I won't have a baby at the end of this."

Sensing he needed to give them privacy, Dawson slipped away almost unnoticed.

Julie sat down in the chair and patted the one beside her. Tabatha eased herself down into it and grunted when she settled.

"I can't say that I know what you're going through because I don't. It's an impossible situation, and I'm so sorry that someone took advantage of you. But I have to tell you that I think you're doing such a courageous thing, giving your baby a chance at the best life possible. So many girls in your situation wouldn't have made it this far."

"Some days, I don't know how I made it this far. I don't know how I'm going to make it after this is over, either."

"Have you thought about maybe getting a counselor?"

"Celeste and Abigail want me to do that. I'm still thinking about it. I'm not so good at sharing my feelings."

"Don't be afraid to get some help. Nobody is going to judge you, Tabatha. None of this was your fault."

"Thank you. Man, my feet and ankles are so swollen today. I really think I could have this baby any day now."

"Well, just know that if you need to go in the house and relax, you are welcome to do that whenever you need. We've got a nice cushy sofa in the living room, bedrooms upstairs..."

"I might actually take you up on that. I don't want to ruin Celeste or Abigail's romantic evening by telling them I want to go home and lay in a hot bath."

"Listen, room four upstairs has the most luxurious jetted tub. If you need to go up there, there are towels in the linen closet in the hallway. Just lock the door, light a candle and enjoy yourself."

She smiled. "Everybody here is so nice. It's made all of this easier."

Julie reached over and squeezed her hand. "Seagrove is a family. We are all *your* family now, Tabatha. You can lean on us. We have your back."

"I have to say, you're a pretty good looking prom date," Abigail said, looking Griffin up and down. They had to work late because a beagle had a chicken bone stuck in the roof of his mouth. The prom was already going, and they were just getting in the car to head over there.

"And you look absolutely stunning," Griffin said, surprising her. There had been little to choose from at the local dress shop, given that just about everybody in town was going to this prom. Abigail had chosen a pretty simple long red dress like something out of a movie. There was nothing particularly special about it, but she was thankful to have the figure to be able to pull it off.

"Thank you. Shall we head that way?"

"Your chariot awaits!"

As they rode over to the inn, which was just a few miles away, they chatted about all kinds of work things. Abigail still wasn't sure if they were actually on a date or if he just needed somebody to go with to the event. Either way, she was happy to have him on her arm.

It had been a long time since she had been out with a man. Her marriage ended in shambles, and her dating life had not been much better. It scared her to give her heart away to anybody else, but she also knew that she didn't want to spend the rest of her life alone.

When they pulled up at the prom, Griffin stepped out of the car and walked around to open the door for her. She couldn't remember the last time a man had done that for her.

"Wow. Real southern chivalry in action," she said, smiling at him.

"My mama taught me right."

"I can see that."

They made their way up to the platform where everybody was dancing and eating. Abigail took two glasses of wine off of a tray and handed one to Griffin.

"I'm starving. Should we make a couple of plates?"

"Absolutely."

"Wow! You *do* have a figure under there," Celeste

said from behind them. Abigail turned around and glared at her.

"And you *are* actually a woman under there."

"Ah, you must be Celeste. I'm Griffin Connor, the new veterinarian in town." He reached out and shook Celeste's hand.

"So, you are Abigail's date tonight, then? I thought you were her boss?"

Abigail wanted to strangle her. "I am her boss, but I needed a date to the prom that some guy was throwing to try to impress his girlfriend."

Celeste smiled. "I like him. He's able to keep up with me. That's a hard thing to do."

"Where is Ben?" Abigail said, trying to change the subject.

"He's around here somewhere. Can you believe he threw a prom for me? Who does that?"

"A very good guy," Abigail said.

"We can agree there. I don't think I've ever met such a good person. Ben is a pediatrician," she said to Griffin.

"I've heard. I'll have to meet him before we leave tonight."

"Well, y'all have fun. I'm going to go do the electric slide."

Abigail watched as Celeste ran off toward the

dance floor, jumping into the middle of a group of people who were stepping sideways and clapping their hands.

"I don't think I've ever seen her this peppy. I mean, she looked almost happy."

"That was happy?"

Abigail laughed. "Celeste is an acquired taste. You just have to get to know her very sarcastic sense of humor. I've learned to live with it."

"You two really do seem like sisters."

"Trust me, that has come after a lot of hard work over the last few months. But I think we understand each other better now, and we have a shared history. It's nice to feel like I have a sister."

"How about we get that food now?"

"Great idea."

CHAPTER 11

JULIE GRINNED WHEN SHE SAW HER DAUGHTER, MEG, and her granddaughter, Vivi, walking in her direction. Christian had to work late, something about an important emergency staff meeting, so Meg had opted to bring her daughter as her date.

Vivi was a little spitfire, running around and getting into everything. She was the pride of Julie's life, and she couldn't wait to have more grandchildren one day. Before then, she would become an aunt when Janine and William adopted any day now. Little kids always brought more life to a family.

These were truly the best times of her life. When her divorce happened, she thought all of her good days were behind her. All the days when her kids were little, and she was the room mom at their school. All of their tennis tournaments, softball games and weekend soccer matches had kept her busy and sane as a young mother, and when those days were over, she'd struggled to feel needed by her kids.

After signing the divorce papers and starting a completely new life, she thought she was going to grow old alone. But now it seemed like she had more happiness and joy in her life than she could've ever expected back in those days.

She had a fantastic husband, a beautiful inn that sat beside the ocean, a variety of wonderful friends surrounding her each day, a great relationship with her sister and her own daughters. There was so much love around her all the time that she was almost overwhelmed.

"Grandma!" Vivi said, as she ran towards her. "Look at my pretty dress!" She twirled around in a circle showcasing the fluffy pink lace tulle dress that Meg had bought her at the dress shop earlier in the day.

"Why, don't you just look like a princess! I think you have the prettiest dress here!"

"You do?" Vivi asked, her eyes wide.

"Absolutely! But we can't tell the other ladies because we don't want them to be sad, right?"

"Right. We don't hurt other people's feelings," Vivi said, reciting what Julie had told her many times. The last thing she wanted was her own granddaughter to become a bully at preschool. Vivi was outspoken, and many times Julie had had to explain to her that words can hurt. She wished the other parents were so careful about teaching their own kids so that Dylan wouldn't have been bullied.

"You look beautiful, Mom," Meg said, commenting on Julie's short gold dress.

"Thank you. I feel like I should be at a New Year's Eve ball drop, but this was really the only thing I liked in the dress store. Who knew that this prom was going to basically deplete all of their inventory?"

"I know. Thankfully, I had this dress from one of our college events." Meg was wearing a simple black dress that came down to her knee with some rhinestones around the neckline.

"You look lovely. So Christian can't come at all tonight?"

"No. Normally he's home hours ago, but they had some kind of emergency staff meeting. Honestly, it didn't sound good. There may be some layoffs."

"Oh no. I hope it's not him. I know y'all are saving for a bigger place."

"Yeah, we were just looking at houses last weekend. I can't wait to find a place that has a big backyard for Vivi, so she can finally get the puppy she wants."

"Puppy!" Vivi said, jumping in the air.

"There's my granddaughter!" Dawson said, walking over and picking her up. Vivi absolutely adored Dawson, and she called him Pops. Julie found that to be adorable. Even though Meg had a father, he'd slowly pulled away from his girls in the last couple of years. It made Julie sad, and she knew it hurt her girls, but they didn't talk about it. It was the giant elephant in the room that no one mentioned.

Dawson had stepped up in a big way as Vivi's grandfather. He saw no difference in her than he did in Dylan. He adored his granddaughter, and Julie knew he would protect her with his life if he had to.

"Hey, Dawson. Don't you look spiffy!"

He looked down at his tuxedo. "I'm ready for my photo shoot. Say, Vivi, do you want to go do a little dancing with your Pops?"

"Yeah, but I'm going to be a better dancer than you," she said, giggling as he tickled her. The two of them walked toward the dance floor.

"She adores him," Meg said, laughing.

"I know, and he loves her to pieces. That's why I'm hoping that this whole thing with Christian's job works out. And yours. I would never want y'all to have to move away for a new job."

"That's what I wanted to tell you, although I wasn't going to mention it at prom."

"What? Tell me."

"I lost my job a few weeks ago. I just didn't want you to worry about us."

Julie put her hands on Meg's arms. "Honey, you should know you can always tell me anything. What happened?"

"Just typical staff cuts. My position was deemed to be unimportant or nonessential, as they called it. I've been looking for something ever since, but no luck so far."

"You know you can always come work at the bookstore. I can cut my hours..."

Meg waved her hand. "No, Mom. I appreciate it. But I'm an adult now, and I'm a mother. I need to handle this by myself."

"I understand. If you need some money, please let me know. Dawson and I have extra, and we would always want to share it with our kids."

Meg reached out and hugged her mother. All Julie could think about was how it didn't matter how old her kids were, they were still her babies. She still always wanted to do everything she could for them, and it was painful to watch them make mistakes or have bad things happen in their lives.

Good mothers always wanted to help. They wanted to fix things, just like little boo-boos kids had when they fell off a bicycle for the first time. To her, Colleen and Meg were still little girls needing her help at every turn.

Sometimes parenting adult children was even harder than parenting little kids.

"You have some pretty great dance moves," Griffin said, laughing as he and Abigail left the dance floor after three songs in a row.

"You're pretty good too. My experience with most men dancing has not been good. I used to date this guy, who looked like he was having some sort of seizure every time he danced. I almost called an ambulance the first time I saw it."

Griffin laughed loudly. They walked over and got a cup of punch and stood at the edge of the dance floor, watching everybody else. Each song they had danced to was a fast one, and now a slow song was playing. Abigail watched the couples swaying back-and-forth in each other's arms and wondered why Griffin hadn't asked her to dance. Maybe this really wasn't a date, as she'd feared. This was just a friend hanging out with another friend.

"This has been a beautiful night. I'm so glad Celeste got to have this experience. I mean, look at her and Ben. They seem perfect for each other," Griffin said.

Abigail looked over at Celeste. With all their history, she was still glad to see her enjoying herself and having somebody pay attention to her like Ben did. At first, she wondered if they were a good match, but he seemed to be able to handle her occasional outbursts and sometimes difficult personality. In fact, he seemed to enjoy it.

"I'm glad too. It's getting kind of late. I don't want to keep you here so that you're exhausted at work tomorrow." A part of her couldn't bear to watch Celeste and Ben, Julie and Dawson, and all the other happy couples staring into each other's eyes. She wanted that for herself, and she seemed to have overestimated Griffin's feelings for her.

"It's a short shift tomorrow. I think we only have three patients."

"Just let me know if you want to leave."

"Do you want to leave?"

"It doesn't matter to me," Abigail said. "I'm enjoying myself."

"Would you be interested in maybe taking a little walk down the beach?"

"Sure, but I'm going to leave these heels here," she said, kicking her shoes off and sliding them under one of the picnic tables.

They walked down the steps and onto the cool sand below. The days were getting warmer, but the nights were still quite cold, especially with the ocean breeze.

"So, how are you liking working at the vet clinic?"

She laughed. "I've only had one shift."

"Did you like it?"

"I did. I love seeing all the animals. My dream one day is to have a little farm where I can have goats, pigs and maybe even some chickens."

"Oh yeah? I never pegged you as a farm girl."

She giggled. "Neither did I. I always thought I would end up in the big city living in some high-rise condo building. But now all I can think about are goats. That might make me insane."

"I think being an animal lover is the most attractive quality in a woman." Suddenly, Abigail got a shiver up her back. Griffin mistook the shiver for the night air, but she knew what it was. This conversation was going to get a lot more personal. "Here, you seem cold," he said, taking off his jacket and wrapping it around her shoulders. Never had anything seemed so sexy in all her life.

"Thanks. It's a little nippy out here tonight."

"I thought I'd miss Nashville, but there's just something about the ocean air, ya know?"

She smiled. "I get it. I remember when I first came back here, Dixie... she runs the bookstore with Julie... she told me one day that when Seagrove gets its hooks in you, you'll never move away."

"I can believe that."

"I honestly didn't believe her at first. I've never been anywhere in my life that I wanted to put down roots until I came to Seagrove."

"I can see myself putting roots down here too."

They walked along quietly for a little while, just the sound of the ocean waves crashing against the shore. Suddenly, a small crab ran across Abigail's path, walking directly over the top of her foot. Without thinking, she literally jumped straight into the air, and Griffin caught her.

"What in the world was that?" she shrieked. Although she loved the beauty of the ocean, she didn't like the critters that lived there.

Griffin started laughing so hard he almost

dropped her. Finally, she slowly climbed down out of his arms, her feet touching the sand and her eyes glued to the ground.

"I think that was a crab."

Abigail laughed. "Sorry about that. I'm not good with bugs, and crabs are basically just ocean bugs."

"I thought you loved all animals?"

"Goats, dogs, cats, maybe even a ferret. But crabs? No, thank you."

"I'll note that. Do you want to sit down for a few minutes?"

"Yes. I need time for my heart to stop fibrillating," she said, clutching her chest as they walked over and sat down on the sand.

"I'm impressed with how quick your reflexes are," he said, chuckling.

"I hope I didn't hurt you when I jumped directly up into your arms. I don't know what I was thinking."

“I’m pretty sure you were thinking that crab was going to kill you."

She nodded. "For a moment, I did think I was going to die."

"You're funny, Abigail. I like that."

There was a long pause, like each of them wasn't sure what to say.

"Can I ask you something?"

"Of course."

"What is this?"

Griffin looked over at her. All she could see was the moonlight dancing off his bluc eyes, and she dared not stare at them very long or possibly make a fool of herself.

"What do you mean?"

"At the risk of sounding like a complete idiot, is this a date?"

Griffin smiled. "Well, I thought it was. But if you don't know, then I must not be doing a very good job."

"I just wasn't sure. I mean, this could've just been two friends keeping each other company at an awkward event. Or it could've been a boss just taking out his new employee."

He held up his hand. "Okay, that last one would've been really creepy and possibly against the law."

"I don't think so, but go ahead..."

"To me, this is a date, Abigail. I took you to the prom. That's, like, serious business," he said, in his best high school boy's voice.

She couldn't help but smile. "So, we're on a date?"

"To summarize, yes, we are definitely on a date. What can I do to prove that to you?"

She shrugged her shoulders. "Letting me jump into your arms when an ocean scorpion ran across my bare feet was a good start."

"Let me try something else." Without missing a beat, he leaned over and pressed his lips to hers. Abigail couldn't think any thoughts. It was like her mind went completely blank and all she could feel was his warm lips against hers. She didn't even care if twenty crabs ran across her feet right now.

Yes, this was most certainly a date. A very, very good date.

Janine tightened her arms around William's neck, pressing her cheek against his chest. Her favorite place to be in the world was in her husband's arms. He wasn't always the best dancer, often stepping on her feet, but she loved this night. It might be one of their last nights as a couple without a child, and she was going to soak it all in.

"You have to admit, I'm doing better. I've only stepped on your foot twice."

Janine giggled. "We've only been dancing for ten minutes, honey."

"Can you believe we will have a baby any day now?"

"No, I can't," she said, looking up at him. "I feel so unprepared. Even though we've got the nursery ready, there's so much more to do!"

He kissed the top of her head. "Don't worry. We'll get everything done. Our baby is going to have the best life."

"I know. I can't wait to do all the fun stuff like mommy and me classes, cuddle sessions in the bed together, and walks around the park."

"Let's not forget late night screaming sessions, poopy diapers, and the occasional screaming fit for no apparent reason."

She pulled back and pinched his cheek. "Don't you try to ruin this for me, William."

"Let me guess, you two are over here talking baby stuff," Julie said, walking up beside them.

"You must be psychic," Janine said. They stopped dancing and moved over to the side of the dance floor to talk to Julie.

"The problem is my wife thinks this is all going to be a bed of roses, and I'm trying to explain to her that there's going to be poop in the middle of the bed of roses."

Julie laughed. "He does have a point. My girls were the apple of my eye, but I didn't sleep for a good four years."

"I'm not going to let either one of you convince me that this won't be perfect. I've waited my whole life for this."

Julie put her arm around her sister. "We're just messing with you, sis. I know you're going to make a fantastic mother, and I can't wait to see you in that role. Of course, I'm going to want to be a very involved aunt."

"Then we'll call you during some of those late night crying sessions, whether it's us or the baby," William said, smiling.

"I really need to go check my phone. I left it in my handbag in the house. The social worker could call at any time, so I've been checking it every thirty minutes."

"I'll come with you," William said.

"No, you wanted to visit with some of your clients over there. Go ahead. I might even sit down for a little while in the house and put up my feet. These shoes are killing me."

"I'd better go find Dawson. There's no telling

where he's gone off to," Julie said, smiling before she walked away, looking for her husband.

Janine watched as William made his way across the dance floor to talk to his clients. She was so happy his business was stable, and hers was as well. This was the perfect time to bring a baby into their family, and she couldn't wait for news from the social worker.

CHAPTER 12

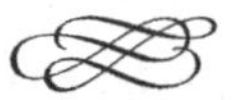

It was official. Tabatha felt like her entire body was about to explode. It was impossible for this to be healthy. How could something grow big enough to make her feel like she was going to pop at any second?

Her skin literally felt like it was about to split open, especially on her feet and ankles. First, she went into the house and sat on the sofa, but then a few people came in, and it made her feel self-conscious. For now, she had settled in the dining room because it had doors that closed.

Lucy, the resident chef and housekeeper at the inn, had offered to make her a cup of tea. Tabatha had gladly taken her up on it, along with a piece of pound cake. If there was one good thing about pregnancy, it was that she could eat as much as she wanted without feeling guilty. Once the baby was born, she would have to be careful again so that she could fit into her clothes.

She leaned back against the chair and propped her feet on another chair across from her. As she finished the last bite of the pound cake, she laid her head back and rested it against the wall that the dining room shared with the living room.

She had no idea if anybody was still out in the living room, but she didn't want to chance it until she was ready to leave the house. It was nice having a little quiet place of our own.

Julie had offered to let her take a bath in the jetted tub upstairs, but she was afraid she wouldn't be able to get herself out once she was finished bathing. Maneuverability was not good for her right now. Sometimes, she sat down and had a hard time getting back up. She could only imagine how hard that would be in a deep tub. Her worst fear was somebody having to call the fire department to extract her out of the bathtub.

She heard a door open, which meant somebody was coming into the house. Glad they couldn't see her, she laid her head back against the wall and closed her eyes.

A few moments later, she recognized the voice. It was Janine, apparently making a phone call.

"Hi. This is Janine. I got your text message. So sorry, I'm at an event and I haven't checked my phone in about half an hour."

"Hi, Janine. Thanks for calling me back so quickly."

Tabatha realized Janine was talking on her speakerphone, as she often did when not many people were around. She told Tabatha she didn't like holding phones up to her ear, something about cancer risks.

"No problem. I've been waiting to hear from you. Do we have good news?"

Tabatha could hear the smile in Janine's voice. She had been so excited about getting news of a baby being born, and Tabatha was happy for her. Janine deserved to be a mother.

"Janine, I don't know quite how to say this."

"To say what?"

"Well, you know the birth mother has been a bit hesitant about meeting you."

"Yes, but we just thought that was jitters. Are you saying she's chosen a different family?"

"Oh no. That's not it at all."

"Oh, good. You scared me for a minute."

Tabatha hated to eavesdrop, but she still found herself pressing her ear against the wall. The old house had thin walls, apparently, because she could hear every word.

"It's just that... the birth mother has decided to... keep her baby."

Tabatha heard silence. Deafening silence. The kind of silence that usually meant somebody had stopped breathing. For a moment, she considered walking through the door and checking on Janine to make sure she hadn't passed out. Thankfully, she spoke before Tabatha had to do that.

"She decided to keep the baby?" Janine echoed, her voice shaking. At that moment, Tabatha wanted to go out and wrap her friend in a big hug. She felt horrible for her.

"She was having a really hard time making the decision, and when she found out she had more family support than she thought, she decided to keep him."

"Him?"

"Her baby boy was born a couple of hours ago."

Tabatha knew Janine must've been devastated because she felt pain in her own heart, and it wasn't even her baby.

"I'm very happy for her. I wish her nothing but the best, and her baby boy."

"I'll make sure to pass that along. She feels very bad about the whole thing."

"Listen, I need to go," Janine said, swallowing hard. Her voice was still shaky.

"I understand. And I will call you as soon as another birth mother picks you."

"You know, let me talk to my husband first. I'm not sure my heart can take much more of this process."

The conversation went silent, so Tabatha could only assume that Janine had ended the call. Then she heard quiet sobs coming from the other side of the wall as she pressed her ear against it. She wanted to go out there, to comfort her, but being pregnant herself, she felt like that would be salt in the wound.

So Tabatha just sat on the other side of the wall, the back of her head leaning against it, as she listened to Janine cry. A few minutes later, the room fell silent, and the door closed. She assumed Janine had dried herself up and re-joined the party.

~

"William, we need to go," Janine said, trying to hurry her husband toward the car. William, looking confused, stared at her.

"Have you been crying?"

"Honey, we really need to go."

"Oh! You just talked to the social worker? Are we supposed to be heading to the hospital?" He said it so loudly that he attracted attention. Julie and Dawson both walked over quickly, big smiles on their faces. Janine wanted to fall to the floor and curl up in the fetal position.

"I talked to the social worker, but she said..."

"Am I about to be an aunt?" Julie asked, clapping her hands together and smiling.

"I think we're heading to the hospital. We should probably run by the house and pick up our bags..."

Janine, frustrated, held up her hands. "Stop it! Just stop! There's no baby for us. I'm not about to be a mother, and you're not about to be a father."

William's face fell, his eyes wide. Julie and Dawson stood there, no words spoken.

"What do you mean?" William finally asked.

"The social worker called. The birth mother decided to keep the baby. It was a boy, not that it matters."

"Oh, Janine. I'm so sorry," Julie said, attempting to hug her sister. Janine pulled away.

"No. Please. I just need to get home."

"Of course. If you need anything, please call us."

Dawson reached over and squeezed William's shoulder. "I'm sorry, man. Things have a way of working out. I'm sure that's what will happen here."

Janine knew that she shouldn't direct her anger at Dawson. After all, he was practically the nicest guy on the planet. But she just couldn't help it.

"You know, it's really easy to say that things work out when they always work out for you and Julie. Things have not worked out for us very well. I'm almost fifty years old, and I still don't have a child. I'm no closer now than I was ten years ago. Please, William, just take me home!"

As they walked to the car, Janine felt a rush of emotions. Devastation. Sadness. Despair. Hopelessness. Embarrassment. All of it was stirred up in a quagmire of feelings that she couldn't seem to separate.

William opened the door, allowing her to sit down in the passenger seat. She crossed her arms over her chest in an effort to protect herself. From what, she didn't know. It felt like everything inside of her had been sucked out. All the hopes and dreams about becoming a mother that she had allowed to build were now gone. There was nothing in their place, and she felt a huge void.

William sat behind the steering wheel, but he didn't move.

“Can we just go home?" Janine repeated.

He looked over at her, hurt painted all over his face. "Can you just give me a minute? I know you're upset, but so am I. This wasn't just your baby, Janine."

At that moment, she felt terrible. Guilt washed over her, obscuring all the other feelings momentarily. She hadn't even been thinking about her poor husband. The man who had painted the nursery, put together the crib and regaled her with stories of the things he was going to do with their new child. He had just as much right to take a moment and grieve for the baby that would never be theirs.

"I'm so sorry, William. I was only thinking about myself."

He reached over and took her hand, squeezing it. "It's okay. I know you're devastated, and so am I. Let's go home, curl up in a blanket and just let ourselves feel sad."

~

Celeste sat at the kitchen table the next morning, well aware that she had had way too many glasses of wine. Her one and only prom had been the best night of her life so far. Having a man who cared so much about her that he would put that kind of effort in was almost overwhelming.

"Pass the sugar, please," Abigail said. Celeste slid it over to her, and Abigail dumped two heaping teaspoons into her cup of coffee. Celeste rolled her eyes.

"I've said it a million times, but you're going to end up diabetic if you don't stop putting so much sugar in your coffee."

Abigail sighed. "Yes, and thank you for repeating it over and over again every single morning of our lives. That is super helpful."

Both of them were exhausted from the night before. "So, how was your date with Griffin?"

Abigail turned all shades of red. "It was good."

"You look like a little schoolgirl right now. What happened?"

"Well, not that it's any of your business, but he took me on a walk on the beach and we might have shared a couple of kisses."

Celeste covered her mouth. "Oh my! A couple of kisses? When is the wedding?"

Abigail glared at her. "Do you have to be sarcastic this early in the morning?"

"Good morning," Tabatha said, padding across the kitchen. If it was possible, she looked even bigger this morning. Celeste expected the baby to just reach its hand straight through her belly button at any moment.

"Good morning. Maybe today is the day," Abigail said, as she did every morning.

"Gosh, I hope so. I can't take this much longer. Even my maternity clothes are tight now. How can a person get this big?" she said, holding out her hands and looking down at her stomach. She was rather large for someone her size.

"It will happen," Celeste said, just trying to say anything to sound like she was in the conversation.

"I'm like eleven months pregnant now. I'm going to call that doctor today and demand they take this baby out if she's not here by tomorrow."

"No, you're not," Celeste muttered under her breath.

Tabatha poured herself a glass of orange juice and sat down at the table. Well, more like plopped down at the table. The chair made a creaking noise, and Celeste was afraid it was going to completely disintegrate underneath her.

"Did you hear about Janine?"

Abigail and Celeste looked at Tabatha. "No. What?"

"Well, I was resting in the dining room at the inn last night when I heard Janine come into the room. She was calling her social worker because apparently she had texted her. Long story short, the birth mother changed her mind about giving her baby up for adoption. Janine was devastated. She doesn't know that I heard."

Abigail covered her mouth. "Oh, my goodness. I feel so bad for them. Janine has been so excited. I ran into her at the department store the other day, and she had a buggy full of baby clothes that would work for any gender."

"It was a little boy," Tabatha said, taking a sip of her juice.

"Well, what about the couple that you chose?" Celeste asked.

"I talked to them on the phone a couple of days ago. They seem nice."

"Do you feel comfortable with the decision about adoption?" Abigail asked. She must've asked her the same question a million times.

"Yes. I've started looking at some colleges, you know, something to look forward to after the baby is born. I don't think I can stay around here and just go back to life like nothing happened. I think I need some new scenery, new people."

"You mean you don't want to live here with us forever?" Celeste asked, laughing.

"Y'all will always be my family. But I need to start over after this. That's why I'm kind of concerned about this couple I chose. They really want me to have a lot of regular interaction and become a member of their family. I'm not sure I'm okay with that."

"Have you told them your wishes?"

"Not yet. I don't know them very well, and it just felt weird to have that conversation. I guess I'll just tell the social worker."

Tabatha looked tired. She had to be nearing the end of her pregnancy any day now because she certainly couldn't continue going on like this. Celeste was truly starting to worry about her.

"Have you thought about who you want in the delivery room?" Abigail asked.

"The doctor said I don't have to have anybody, or I could have a midwife or something. But I was thinking about asking Janine."

Celeste's eyes got wide. "Janine? I don't think that's a good idea."

"Well, to be fair, I thought she was going to have a baby by the time I gave birth. I was kind of interested in her being in the delivery room because she's been teaching me these special breathing techniques. Since I didn't go to birthing classes, I thought she might be a good choice."

"One of us could be with you," Abigail offered.

Tabatha smiled. "I appreciate it. And I love you guys. But neither one of you have had a baby, and Janine knows all kinds of breathing techniques. I'm sure this is going to hurt, and I would like to minimize my pain as much as possible."

"Is she even working today?" Celeste asked.

"I don't know. I thought I would take a walk over to the yoga studio and see if she's there. She might have taken the day off, or she may be one of those people who wants to distract herself with work. Yoga and meditation are how she deals with things."

Janine stood in the middle of her yoga studio, unsure of why she was even there. Her heart certainly wasn't in it today, and she always liked to give her best to her students. But sitting home today just wasn't an option. William had a boat tour he couldn't cancel, so she would've been sitting alone, trying to avoid going into her empty nursery.

Of course, Julie and Dixie had both offered to come over and keep her company, but she didn't really feel like entertaining anyone. She just wanted to keep her head down, teach her students, and then fall into her husband's arms at the end of the day.

The night before had been filled with so much joy, followed by so much sorrow. Such is life, she supposed. She and William had stayed up most of the night talking, with Janine sobbing off and on more times than she could count.

Still, she knew she was blessed, and the light of day had brought a renewed hope. Maybe she would become a mother, and this baby wasn't meant to be hers. God obviously had something else in mind. That didn't make it hurt any less, though.

"Janine?"

She turned to see a very pregnant Tabatha standing in the doorway of the studio. "Oh, sorry. I didn't hear you come in. Do we have a session today?"

"No. Sorry to come unannounced."

"Glad to see you," she said, walking closer. "Girl, you look like you might pop any second."

Tabatha smiled. "I feel that way, too. Listen, can we talk?"

"Sure." Janine pointed to a small sofa on the other side of the room. Her students often sat there chatting after class.

"First, I want to say how sorry I am about the adoption falling through."

Janine was surprised. "How did you know about that?"

"I was in the dining room while you were on the phone with the social worker. I didn't want to interrupt, so I heard the whole thing."

She nodded. "Yeah, it was pretty shocking news."

Tabatha squeezed her hand. "I know you must be really upset. It's okay to talk about it. I know I'm this giant pregnant reminder, but I think of you as my friend. I mean, even if you are old enough to be my mother."

Janine laughed. "Thanks. It is very upsetting. We had our hopes up. I should learn not to allow myself to get so carried away, I guess."

"You had every right to be excited."

She swiped at a stray tear rolling down her cheek. "So, Julie tells me you've chosen a family for your baby. They must be so excited."

Tabatha shrugged her shoulders. "That's not set

in stone yet, actually. They want more than I'm willing to give as far as involvement. I'm still thinking about it."

"Well, you need to make the decision that's right for you and your baby."

"I came by here to ask you for a favor, and I hope you don't get offended or upset with me."

"What?"

"Since you've been coaching me on breathing techniques, I was wondering if you'd be open to being my birth partner?"

Janine stared at her for a long moment like she was surprised. "Really?"

"Yes. I mean, I'd totally understand if you said no given what you're going through..."

"I'd love to!" Janine smiled broadly.

"You would?"

"Of course! I've always wanted to be in the room when a baby was born, but I never got the chance to do that. It would be an honor to coach you through your birth, Tabatha. Truly."

"Thank you. Now I don't feel so alone. I'm getting more scared now that I know the birth is coming soon. I made the mistake of watching a video of this woman giving birth, and it was like something out of a horror movie."

Janine laughed. "Don't worry. I'm going to do some research on how to make the room as calm and soothing as possible for you. It'll give me something to distract myself."

"So, I guess I'll need to give Celeste and Abigail your cell phone number so they can call you when we head to the hospital."

"Yes, and I will keep my volume turned up no matter what time of day. This is so exciting."

Tabatha smiled, but inside, she didn't feel excited. The day was drawing closer when she'd have to say goodbye to her baby and start her life over again. She didn't feel settled about it at all. On the one hand, she wanted to be able to see her baby sometimes, just to make sure she was okay. On the other hand, she wasn't sure she wanted constant contact with the family she chose because she didn't think she could start fresh with that much involvement.

One thing was for sure - her baby was coming soon no matter what she did, and choices would have to be made.

CHAPTER 13

"Are you sure you're okay with that?" Julie asked her sister as they sat outside the cafe having lunch.

"I'm very sure. I can't do anything about what happened with our birth mother, but I can support Tabatha through this difficult ordeal. Maybe it will give me more insight into what our birth mother was thinking."

"I need to ask you something, and I'm afraid you'll get mad at me."

Janine looked into Julie's eyes. "No, I am not doing this hoping Tabatha will give us her baby."

"I didn't want to assume…"

"She's chosen a family, Julie. I would never interfere with that. I just want to help her."

"Okay. Well, I'm glad she has you."

"Hey, ladies. Mind if I join you?" Dixie asked, walking over to the table.

"Sure. Have a seat," Janine said, patting the chair next to her.

"Aren't you supposed to be running our book-store?" Julie asked with a laugh.

"Eh, it was slow anyhow. I put a sign on the door. How're you doing, honey?"

Janine sighed. "I go back and forth between hope and sobbing. How are you?"

"I'm sad. I had breakfast with William, and I know he's hurting too."

"He is. We talked about it all night. I'm pretty exhausted today."

"I know things are going to work out, Janine. Some other birth mother is going to choose you and William very soon," Julie said, taking a sip of her sweet tea.

"I don't know if I can do this again. I got my hopes up so high, and the fall was really hard. Maybe I'm just not meant to be a mommy."

"That's not true, darlin'. God just had some other plan, and we don't always understand what it is," Dixie said, rubbing her arm.

"Janine is going to be Tabatha's birth coach."

Dixie paused for a moment, not making eye

contact. "You think that's a good idea, dear?"

"I do. I've been helping her with breathing techniques, and she has no one else who can do that. I want to make this an easier experience for her."

"You know she's found a family for her baby already, right?" Dixie asked.

Janine smiled at her. "I know. I promise I won't run away with her."

"We won't see you on the news?"

Janine chuckled. "No, you won't see me on the news. I'm really okay. I'll get over this, but I just need some time to grieve, I guess."

Julie and Dixie both reached across the table and took her hands. "Just remember that we're always here for you," Julie said.

Dixie smiled. "That's right. You're not getting rid of us, no matter what you do."

Abigail was starting to second-guess her decision to have Griffin over for dinner. Celeste had insisted they do a double date, and Ben was cooking steaks on the grill. They had invited Tabatha to join them, but she preferred to stay in her bedroom with her feet up on a pillow. She was way too uncomfortable to enjoy a big dinner party.

"I can't believe that you talked me into this," Abigail said as she washed the lettuce.

"It's a date. What's the big deal?"

"Our thing is so new. I mean, we kissed, but it doesn't mean we're dating."

"It's just dinner. You act like I invited him over for an impromptu wedding."

Abigail laughed. "I never know what you're going to do. You could absolutely have a reverend hiding in the back."

They continued preparing the meal, Ben out next to the grill, getting the steaks ready. Celeste has been marinating them all day in some kind of concoction that Ben created.

Abigail handled the salad while Celeste was handling the baked potatoes and the "fixings".

"I guess we can make a plate and take it up to Tabatha," Celeste said.

"Yeah, she'd probably like to have a little something, at least a potato. I'm not sure if she could fit a steak in her body."

"I can't believe Janine said yes. I'm glad, of course."

"Me too. I know it's going to be hard for her, but

Tabatha can really use the support in the delivery room."

They continued getting dinner ready and set the table. Griffin arrived, and Abigail welcomed him at the door. To her surprise, he leaned down and gave her a quick kiss. It seemed so easy and natural, like they'd been together a long time.

"Come on in," Abigail said, blushing a bit.

Griffin held out a bottle of wine. "I didn't know what to bring, and I figured wine is always a good choice."

Abigail laughed. "After as much as I drank at the prom, I'm not sure I ever want to see a glass of wine again."

They went into the kitchen, and Ben asked how everybody wanted their steaks cooked. They made their way out onto the deck and stood around the grill chatting and laughing. Abigail couldn't remember a time when she felt so comfortable with a group of people, and she couldn't believe one of them was Celeste.

Just as Ben was getting the steaks off the grill, they heard somebody yelling from inside the house. Celeste and Abigail ran inside quickly and saw Tabatha standing at the bottom of the stairs, gripping the handrail, a puddle of water between her feet.

"Hey guys... It seems that I might be in labor..." she said, frozen like a deer in front of headlights.

A flurry of activity happened around her. Abigail immediately called Janine, who said she would meet them at the hospital. Celeste ran upstairs and grabbed Tabatha's bag while Ben and Griffin helped her to the car. A few minutes later, they were already on their way to the hospital.

"These contractions hurt!" Tabatha said, gripping Abigail's petite hand and almost breaking it.

Somehow, she had been elected to sit in the backseat next to Tabatha, and she was thinking her hand might not survive. Ben was driving the car while Celeste sat beside him. Griffin followed them in his car.

"It looks like your contractions are about eight minutes apart," Celeste said, looking at her phone.

"What does that mean?" Tabatha asked.

Celeste looked over at Ben as if she was hoping he had a better answer.

"The closer they are together, the closer you are to giving birth," Ben said, driving a little faster.

"Just breathe," Abigail said, having no other advice to give her.

It seemed like hours, but they were at the hospital within ten minutes. Ben pulled up to the door, Celeste jumped out and ran inside, and two nurses came out with a wheelchair immediately. Before they knew it, Tabatha was wheelcd away to the back, and they were relegated to sitting in the waiting room like husbands from the fifties.

Janine ran down the hallway and finally found the room. Tabatha was already in the bed wearing a gown, and she was holding onto the railing for dear life.

"I'm here, I'm here!" Janine said, running into thc room.

"Thank goodness. These contractions are very painful. They said they are about five minutes apart now. Something about being six inches dilated?"

"You're doing great. Did they give you an epidural?"

"They tried. It only numbed half of my body."

Janine pulled up a chair and held her hand. "Let's do some breathing exercises."

For the next few minutes, Janine worked with her to calm herself down and breathe through the pain. Tabatha seemed a lot more serene once she got the hang of it.

"Thank you for coming. I didn't expect to go into labor so quickly after we talked."

"I'm glad to be here. Witnessing a birth is going to be such a blessing. I never thought I would get to do such a thing."

"One day, you'll have a baby girl who will grow up and have her own kids. I'm sure you'll get to see their births."

Janine thought it was an odd statement. "I love your optimism, and I hope you're right. For now, let's focus on you and that beautiful little baby, okay?"

Tabatha was getting tired, sweat beading on her brow, and pain etched on her face. It was hard to watch.

"How much longer?" Tabatha asked, writhing around. Thankfully, the nurse came in at just the right moment to check on her.

"Let me take a look, hon," she said in a soothing tone. "Looks like you're almost there, sweetie."

"Good," she said, groaning as another contraction hit. The epidural didn't seem to be helping at all.

The nurse went to find the doctor, and Janine focused her attention back on Tabatha. "You know, most first pregnancies take a lot longer. You're progressing quickly, which is a good thing."

"It doesn't feel quick. Don't tell Abigail and Celeste, but I'd been having contractions all day, and I didn't tell them."

"What? Why?"

"They were having a double date and cooking steaks. I didn't want to ruin it. Plus, I was more comfortable in my own bed."

"Well, we're here now, and everything is going to be okay. Now, breathe…."

"I really wish I'd grabbed those steaks," Ben whispered to Celeste.

"I know. I'm starving, and that vending machine over there is less than appetizing."

"What is taking so long?" Abigail asked, pacing between the chairs.

"It's been half an hour. Calm down," Celeste said, rolling her eyes. "She could be in there for hours and hours."

Abigail sat down, and Griffin took her hand. "She's going to be fine."

"How is she?" Julie asked, as she breezed through the door.

"No updates yet. Janine is in with her, though."

"Good. I can't wait for her to be done with all this. She looked miserable, poor thing. No sixteen-year-old should have to go through what she has."

They waited in silence, with the TV playing in the background. Some home renovation show was on, but nobody was watching it. Celeste pulled out a crossword puzzle book while Abigail stared off into space. Julie read a book, and Ben answered emails on his phone. Griffin just sat and held Abigail's hand.

"Are you the family of Tabatha?" A nurse finally appeared in the small waiting room, and everything turned around.

"Yes, we are," Celeste said confidently.

"Janine asked me to come update you. She's nearing the end of labor and should be giving birth any time now."

"Oh, wonderful," Julie said before the nurse walked away.

"Maybe we should say a prayer for an easy, quick birth experience?" Ben offered. Everyone nodded, sat up at the edge of their chairs, and closed their eyes. Tabatha needed all the help she could get.

Tabatha breathed in and out, in and out. The breath work was definitely helping, and she was thankful to have Janine with her. It would've felt very lonely to give birth all by herself in a cold hospital room with strangers.

"Focus on your breathing," Janine reminded. The doctor and the nurse had already put her feet in the stirrups and draped her legs with a sheet. Everything was ready for her daughter to make her appearance.

Tabatha had never been so scared in her life. Not only did she have a low tolerance for pain, but she was going to be giving her baby away. That alone felt like the worst dagger through her heart. She knew she was making the right decision, both for herself and the baby, but that didn't make it any easier.

"It looks like we're ready to start pushing," the doctor said.

Tabatha had been feeling the urge to push for a while now, but they had told her not to do it until she was fully dilated. Now is the time. Her daughter would be in her arms within minutes, and she didn't know how she would ever let her go.

"Okay, push, Tabatha!"

She pushed down harder than she ever had in her

life. Janine held her hand and kept coaching her, wiping her brow with a cold cloth.

"Okay, stop. Take a few breaths and relax until the next contraction."

"You're doing great," Janine said in a soothing voice.

"I don't think I can do this!"

"Yes, you can. You're strong. You're doing good."

The next contraction rolled over her like a freight train. "Okay, time to push again!"

Tabatha pushed as hard as she could, giving up halfway through it and leaning her head back against the pillow. "I can't. I just can't."

"You have to push, Tabatha. The baby's head is almost out," the doctor said.

The contraction faded away, and Tabatha took a few breaths before the next one hit. She pushed as hard as she could and felt the baby's head pop out.

"Her shoulders are a little stuck because you're so small, so I'm going to have to maneuver a bit. You might feel some pressure."

Pressure was an understatement. She felt like her whole lower half was being ripped apart. How did women do this without any drugs at all? She never wanted to find out.

A few moments later, she heard the sound of a

baby crying and then saw the doctor stand up, holding her in her arms. Tabatha felt frozen in time. She stared between her knees, looking at the baby, and wondered how she was ever going to let her go.

The doctor handed the baby to the nurse, and the nurse quickly cleaned her up before bringing her to Tabatha. She had never held a baby before and wasn't sure how to do it, so Janine helped her.

The next thing she knew, she was looking into her baby's eyes. She was so alert and real. She looked a lot like Tabatha had seen in her own baby pictures with porcelain white skin, bright blue eyes and not a hair on top of her head.

"Oh, my gosh. She's so cute," Tabatha said, feeling the sting of warm tears falling down her face.

"She's beautiful," Janine said, wiping tears away from her own eyes.

"I can't believe I just had a baby."

"I'm going to let you two have some time together," Janine said, turning toward the door.

"Why don't you hold her?"

"What? No. This is your time with your daughter before..."

"I know. But you helped me bring her into this world. Here, hold her."

Janine carefully reached out and picked up the

baby, cradling her in her arms. She smiled down at her. "Aren't you a beautiful little thing? You're going to have such a wonderful life." It warmed Tabatha's heart to see her baby in Janine's arms.

"She really is."

Janine looked at Tabatha. "So, do you feel better about your choice for the adoptive family?"

"Yes. I finally feel at peace about it."

"Should I call the social worker? Does she even know that you're here?"

Tabatha pulled the blanket up around her chest area. "No. There's no need to call her."

"Why not? She needs to alert the adoptive family so they can come to the hospital and sign papers. I mean, unless you plan to take the baby home for a few days?"

Tabatha shook her head. "No. The baby won't be leaving the hospital with me. She'll be leaving the hospital with you."

It took Janine a moment to realize what Tabatha had said. She stared at her. "What?"

"God had a plan when he stopped the adoption with the other birth mother you had. I never felt comfortable with a couple I chose, and they wanted a lot more from me than I was willing to give. I need to be able to start my life over and know that my daughter is safe and loved. And I want to be able to see her from time to time, but I don't want to constantly be in her life confusing her."

"What are you saying, Tabatha?"

"I'm saying that you're holding your daughter, Janine."

Janine's eyes filled with tears. "You can't do this. I don't want you to feel like I pressured you..."

"You didn't pressure me. And if you don't want to go through with this, I'll understand. You have the right to say no. But I would greatly like it if you would be my daughter's mother."

"Really? This is my daughter?"

"Yes. I just ask that you love her and protect her for the rest of your life."

Janine looked down at her new baby and smiled. "It would be my honor."

EPILOGUE

TODAY WAS JANINE'S PROUDEST DAY. HER BABY GIRL, Madison, had just been dedicated at the local church. She and William had stood before God and their family and friends, and promised to raise her in a godly home.

Madison had worn a beautiful pink dress, although her tiny body was swallowed up by it. She was only three months old, but she was the center of Janine and William's world.

"It's my turn to hold her," SuAnn said, holding out her arms. "Dixie held her for a good half hour. Grandmothers have rights."

Janine rolled her eyes and handed the baby over to her mother. "You'd better bring her back in a few minutes. She'll be ready for a bottle."

"I can feed her, Janine. I fed you and Julie just fine, didn't I?" She took the diaper bag from Janine's shoulder and slipped away into the inn where she could hide from everyone and love on Madison for as long as she wanted.

Julie and Dawson were kind enough to host a picnic for family and close friends. It was a beautiful day with clear blue skies and warm temperatures. Now that summer was upon them, the temperatures and humidity would go higher and higher. Janine loved it since she was perpetually cold.

"Where's my niece?" Julie asked, handing Janine a cup of fruit punch.

"Mom stole her, as usual."

Julie laughed. "Dixie will find her soon enough. Don't worry. Those two are like dogs fighting over a bone."

"The hamburgers are almost done," Dawson said as he walked over. "And I made some hotdogs for the kids. Dylan only eats hotdogs."

"I don't know where William went," Janine said, looking around.

"Oh, he went with Ben and Griffin to look at the new dock I built down the beach."

"New fishing place?"

"Of course!"

"Have you heard from Tabatha lately?" Julie asked.

Janine nodded. "Yes. I hear from her about once every couple of weeks. She finally asked for some pictures of Madison, which I was happy to give her. She's settling in Savannah very nicely, and I think she starts summer classes soon."

Tabatha had turned seventeen just after Madison was born, and she was able to get permission to go take some core college classes in Savannah. Abigail and Celeste had signed on as her official foster parents so she still had guardians watching over her. They wanted her to feel like she still had a real family.

"That's wonderful. I'm so glad she's doing well."

"I always tell her to come visit anytime. I want Madison to know her. The more people who love her, the better. I don't know if Tabatha will ever be totally ready, but the door is always open."

"Where's my grandbaby?" Dixie asked, walking up with a giant sun hat on her head.

"Our mom swept her away into the inn."

Dixie pursed her lips. "She's my friend, but I just might sock her in the jaw before this day is over," she muttered as she slow jogged to the side entrance of the house.

"Thanks for inviting us," Abigail said as she joined the group.

"You're always welcome! Friends are family in Seagrove," Julie said, smiling. "Where's Celeste?"

Abigail rolled her eyes. "She bet Ben and Griffin that she could throw a football farther than them, so I think they're on the beach."

Everyone laughed. Janine smiled as she looked around her group of friends and family. Even Emma, who ran the lighthouse, had shown up to see the new baby and eat with them. Colleen had joined by video to see the dedication at the church. Meg, Vivi, and Christian were sitting at a nearby picnic table, eating potato chips while the hamburgers finished cooking.

Her circle of love was strong and all-encompassing, and now she got to share that with her new baby daughter. Tabatha had given her the best gift life could offer, and she would forever be grateful to be called a mother.

Visit my website at www.RachelHannaAuthor.com to see all of my books!

Made in the USA
Coppell, TX
16 May 2022